DARREN SHAN

ZOM-B

BABY

LITTLE, BROWN AND COMPANY   NEW YORK BOSTON

Text copyright © 2013 by HOME OF THE DAMNED LIMITED
Illustrations copyright © 2013 by Warren Pleece

Little, Brown and Company

Hachette Book Group
237 Park Avenue, New York, NY 10017
Visit our website at www.lb-teens.com

Little, Brown and Company is a division of Hachette Book Group, Inc.
The Little, Brown name and logo are trademarks of Hachette Book Group, Inc.

The publisher is not responsible for websites (or their content)
that are not owned by the publisher.

First Edition: October 2013
First printed in Great Britain by Simon & Schuster in 2013

Library of Congress Cataloging-in-Publication Data

Shan, Darren.
  Zom-B baby / Darren Shan.—First edition.
     pages cm.—(Zom-B ; [5])
  Summary: "Grateful for the company of the Angels, B nevertheless questions their mission to eradicate the living dead from the face of the earth, and encounters a horror beyond imagining"—Provided by publisher.
     ISBN 978-0-316-21420-9 (hardcover : alk. paper)—ISBN 978-0-316-21419-3 (e-book)—ISBN 978-0-316-25472-4 (e-book library edition)   [1. Zombies—Fiction.
2. London (England)—Fiction.   3. England—Fiction.   4. Horror stories.]   I. Title.
  PZ7.S52823Zn 2013
  [Fic]—dc23

                                                                           2012051398

10   9   8   7   6   5   4   3   2   1

RRD-C

Printed in the United States of America

For:
She's slim and trim,
And not my mother,
It's Rosie Brock,
Could be no other!

OBE (Order of the Baby's Entrails) to:
Hallie Patterson, for nursing me through a
top-notch tour

Editorial mummies:
Venetia Gosling
Kate Sullivan

Crèche services arranged by the Christopher
Little Agency

DEATH'S SHADOW

WOLF ISLAND

DARK CALLING

HELL'S HEROES

THE CIRQUE DU FREAK SERIES

A LIVING NIGHTMARE

THE VAMPIRE'S ASSISTANT

TUNNELS OF BLOOD

VAMPIRE MOUNTAIN

TRIALS OF DEATH

THE VAMPIRE PRINCE

HUNTERS OF THE DUSK

ALLIES OF THE NIGHT

KILLERS OF THE DAWN

THE LAKE OF SOULS

LORD OF THE SHADOWS

SONS OF DESTINY

THEN…

When zombies rampaged through London on the day that the world fell, Becky Smith ended up trapped in her school. Having been cornered by the brain-hungry beasts, her heart was ripped from her chest and she became one of the living dead.

After months of mindless mayhem, she recovered her senses in an underground complex. She found out that there were two types of zombies—reviveds and revitalizeds. The latter could think and reason the way they had when they were alive, but they had to keep eating brains or they'd become hollow-minded reviveds again.

The revitalized teenagers in the complex referred to themselves as zom heads. They were being held prisoner by a group of scientists and soldiers. B hated being one of their lab rats, and refused to play along with their experiments. To punish her, they stopped feeding her, and she waited for her brain to shut down again.

Before B regressed, a nightmarish clown, Mr. Dowling, invaded with a team of mutants, attacked the humans and freed the undead. B and another zom head called Rage managed to escape. B wandered the streets of London for a time, surviving on any scraps of brain that she could find in the many corpses littering the ruined city. During her travels she met an artist, Timothy Jackson, who believed God had given him the task of painting pictures of the zombies, so that future generations would have a record of the atrocities.

After another run-in with soldiers and the mutants, a broken, lonely B wound up at County Hall, where the centenarian Dr. Oystein offered her refuge. He was one of the few adult revitalizeds in the world. The kindly scientist had established a base for undead, conscious teenagers like B. He referred to them as Angels and, like the artist Timothy, believed that he was on a mission from God.

Dr. Oystein told B that he was the very first revitalized, that God had directly intervened to restore his senses, that he was working to save the world, under orders from the Almighty. As a baby, B had been vaccinated by one of Dr. Oystein's nurses, as had all of the other revitalizeds. The vaccine was the reason they had recovered their senses.

But Dr. Oystein hadn't saved the children to be charitable. He needed them to fight in a war. As B listened with a mixture of disbelief and horror, he told her that while he was an agent for a force of universal goodness, Mr. Dowling was a being of universal evil. If the clown's army overcame Dr. Oystein's Angels, the world would topple into a dark abyss and every survivor would fall prey to his foul, hellish servants.

ONE

NOW...

The London Dungeon used to be one of the city's top tourist attractions. It was a fun but grisly place, a cross between a museum and a horror house. It re-created some of London's darker historical moments, bringing back to life the world of people like Jack the Ripper and Swee-ney Todd. It featured sinister, imposing models of buildings from the past, props like hanging skeletons and snarling rats, nerve-tingling videos and light shows, and actors to play the various infamous figures. There were even some stomach-churning rides. I visited it quite a few times when I was alive, and always had a brilliant time.

I haven't been in the Dungeon since returning to County Hall as a revitalized, but right now it feels like the most natural part of the complex to head for.

I wander through the deserted rooms, enjoying the isolation and the gloominess. The actors are gone, and someone must have done the rounds and turned off all the projectors and video clips, but most of the lights work, and the sets and props haven't been disturbed. It's still the coolest damn place in London.

I also think, looking back, that it served as a taste of what was to come. The London Dungeon painted a picture of a blood-drenched city full of terror and murder, and the people who built it were right—this *is* a realm of madness and death. We were never more than one sharp twist away from total chaos, from demonic clowns prancing through the streets and tenderhearted but loopy scientists setting themselves up as spokesmen for God.

I thought I'd escaped the craziness when I came to County Hall. London had been destroyed, zombies had taken over, life as we knew it had come to an end. But Dr. Oystein seemed to offer sanctuary from the grim bedlam of the streets. I thought I could rest easy, make friends, learn from the good doctor, start to build a new life (or should that be *un*life?) for myself.

That was before the doctor told me that God speaks to him.

I creep along a street that looks like it's been transported to the present day from Victorian London. I pause, imagining banks of swirling fog, waiting for Jack the Ripper to leap out and claim me for his own. That's not very likely, I know, but it wouldn't surprise me. I reckon just about anything could happen in this crazy, messed-up world.

That's what's so weird and scary about the story Dr. Oystein fed us. There was a time when I would have written him off as a kook, but given what I've seen and experienced recently, I can't say for sure that he *is* barking mad. He told me he was forced by Nazis to create the zombie gene—that's probably fact. It's clear that he's an expert on the living dead, having studied them for decades. He's the one who gave me the ability to revitalize.

If all that and more is true, then why not the rest of it? The world has always been full of people claiming to be in contact with God. Surely they can't *all* have been nutters. If some of them were the genuine article, maybe Dr. Oystein is too. The trouble is, how's an ordinary girl like me to supposed to be able to tell the difference between a prophet and a madman?

I curse loudly and slam a fist into one of the fake walls, punching a large hole through it. Someone chuckles behind me.

"Now *there's* a cliché if ever I saw one."

I turn and glare at Rage, who has followed me in from the riverbank. Mr. Burke is with him. Rage is sneering. Burke just looks uncomfortable.

"Why don't you go drown yourself?" I snarl at Rage.

"I would if I could," he smirks, then pokes his chest. "I'm the same as you. My lungs don't work."

3

I had left Rage, Burke and Dr. Oystein abruptly, without saying anything, once the doctor had hit us with the revelation that he was God's envoy, locked in battle with Mr. Dowling, aka the literal spawn of Satan. I couldn't take any more. My head was bursting.

"I haven't been in this part of the building before," Burke says, looking around.

"This was the London Dungeon," I tell him.

My ex-teacher nods. "I often meant to check it out, but I never got around to it."

"I came here lots," I sniff. "My mum hated the place, but Dad was like me, he thought it was great. He'd bring me here, just the two of us, and we'd have a wicked time."

"I bet," Burke says.

"What's that supposed to mean?" I shout, thinking he's having a dig at my racist dad, implying that he liked the horrors of the Dungeon because he was horrific himself.

Burke blinks, startled by my tone. "Nothing. It looks like it must have been a lot of fun back in the day. That's all I was saying."

Rage snorts. "Always thought the Dungeon was rubbish myself."

I laugh shortly. "That's because you're a moron with no taste."

"Yeah," he says. "That must be why I fancy you."

I give him the finger, but chuckle despite myself.

"So what do you think of old Oystein's story?" Rage asks.

I shrug and look away.

"He's off his head, isn't he?" Rage pushes.

4

"I suppose..."

"Do you think any of it was real? Being imprisoned by the Nazis, inventing the zombie gene, working with governments and armies all these years to suppress breakouts?"

"Those are undeniable facts," Burke says quietly. "I discussed Dr. Oystein with my military contacts when I was leading a double life. Everything he told us today checked out."

"What about his direct line to God?" Rage jeers.

Burke sighs. "That's where we hit a gray area."

"Nothing gray about it," Rage says cheerfully. "The doc's a lunatic. I don't believe in God, the Devil, reincarnation, nothing like that. Even if I did, his story doesn't ring true. The all-powerful creator of the universe teaming up with a brain-hungry zombie? Get real!"

"Many prophets were outcasts of their time," Burke murmurs. "They were mistrusted and feared by their contemporaries, mocked, abused, driven from their homes. Christ was crucified, John the Baptist's head was chopped off, Joan of Arc was burned at the stake."

"Yeah," Rage says, "but they were human, weren't they? They were alive."

"Lazarus," I say softly, the memory coming to me out of nowhere. "Jesus raised him from the dead. The first zombie."

Rage starts to laugh, then considers what I've said and frowns. "You think the doc's telling the truth?"

I pull a face. "How the hell do I know? It sounds crazy, but..."

"I don't do *buts*," Rage says. "It's a simple world as long as you don't let others complicate it for you. The doc's a genius, no one's denying that, but he's mad too. I respect him for the Groove Tubes, bringing the Angels together and all the rest, but I'm not gonna pretend there wasn't steam coming out of his ears when he started telling us about his cozy chats with God."

"So what are you gonna do?" I ask.

"About what?"

"This war he wants us to fight. The Angels versus Mr. Dowling and his army of mutants. If you don't believe God's on our side, or that we're fighting the forces of darkness, where does that leave you?"

"Right where I want to be," Rage smirks. "In the thick of it all."

He walks up to the plasterboard wall I punched and studies the hole I made.

"We're built to fight," he whispers, rubbing together the bones sticking out of his fingers. "We were reborn as perfect killing machines. I always wanted to join an army. I had it all planned. I was gonna give myself a couple of years after school to see the world, have some laughs, sow my wild seeds."

"Oats," Burke corrects him.

"Whatever. Then I was gonna join the French Foreign Legion or something like that. Go where the battles were, test myself on the field of combat, maybe become a mercenary further down the line, hire myself out to whoever paid me the most."

"You don't believe in loyalty to a cause?" Burke asks diplomatically.

"Loyalty's for mugs," Rage says.

Burke looks disappointed. "Then you're not going to stay with Dr. Oystein?"

Rage frowns. "Weren't you listening? I want to be where the action is. Dr. Oystein's five cans short of a six-pack, but if he's gonna start a war with the clown and his mutants, I want to be there when they clash. So, yeah, I'm his man if he'll have me."

"You're going to stay even though you think Dr. Oystein is mad?" I gape.

"Of course," Rage says calmly. "War's in my blood. I want to be a warrior and Oystein's offering me the best fight in town. Why would I turn my back on the chance to go toe-to-toe with an army of mutants and their diabolical leader? Hell, if we win, I might end up saving the world from the Devil—how ironic would that be, given that I don't even believe in the bugger?"

Rage turns to leave.

"And what if the Devil makes you a better offer?" Burke asks.

Rage looks back uncertainly.

"What if Mr. Dowling asks you to join him somewhere down the line?" Burke presses. "Would you consider a proposal from our enemy?"

"Might do," Rage nods. "Offhand I can't think of anything he could offer to tempt me, since money doesn't mean anything these days. But never say never, right?"

"You'd sell us out?" I shout.

"In a heartbeat," Rage says, then flashes his teeth in a merciless grin. "God, the Devil, forces in between...It makes no difference to me. I'll go where the going's good. Right now I'm best off sticking with Dr. Oystein. But I'm not in this game to save the world or what's left of mankind. I'm just a guy in search of some kicks to pass the time before my tired old bones give up the ghost."

Rage cocks his head and grunts. "If the doc's right about us being able to survive for thousands of years, that's a lot of time to play with. I'll need a lot of kicks. Maybe spend a century working for the good guys, then a century for the villains. Or take on the whole lot of you together—Rage against the world. Wherever the opportunity for the most excitement lies, that's where you'll find me.

"Take care, folks. And watch your backs."

Then, with a laugh, he's gone, leaving Burke and me to stare at each other in openmouthed disbelief.

TWO

"Maybe you were right," Burke mutters. "We might have been better off if we'd killed him when he was in the Groove Tube."

I chuckle. "You don't really mean that."

"No," he smiles. "I suppose I don't. But I'll have to keep a close watch on him. I hadn't realized he was this dangerous."

"The clue was in the name," I note drily.

Burke winces. "It's always a dark day when the student becomes the teacher. Especially a student as limited as you were. No offense."

"Get stuffed."

We laugh, and for a while it's like we're back in school, just a cool teacher and a teenage girl sharing a joke.

"So what do *you* think of the whole Dr. Oystein and God thing?" I ask.

Burke sighs. "Does it matter?"

"Of course it does."

"Why?" he challenges me. "Isn't faith a personal choice? Don't we all listen to our hearts and choose to believe – or not – based on what we feel rather than on what other people tell us?"

"No," I snort. "We believe whatever our parents tell us, until we're old enough to decide for ourselves. Then most of us go along with what we grew up with because it's easier than trying to learn something new."

Burke claps enthusiastically. "My star student. Why did you never come up with airtight reasoning like that in class?"

"Because school was boring," I tell him.

"Ouch," he says, then sighs again. "You're right, of course. But whether we choose to believe or just stick with the faith we've grown up with, the truth is that nobody can ever say for sure if there's a God or not. Dr. Oystein is convinced that there is, and for all I know he's right."

"But if he's not?" I press.

"I don't think it matters." Burke grimaces. "I mean, under different circumstances I'd be wary of him. Lots of wars have been fought by people who used religion as an excuse. Kings, politicians and generals twisted the beliefs of their followers as they saw fit, playing the religious card to justify their crusades over land, oil, gold or whatever it was they were really fighting for."

"Isn't that what Dr. Oystein is doing?" I ask.

"I don't think so. He's asking us only to have faith in him, not in his God, to accept that he's working in the name of good, to overcome the forces of darkness that are stacked against us. Whatever you think about God, nobody can deny that we're facing dark times. The zombies, Mr. Dowling and his mutants... These are forces we can't ignore, enemies that have to be faced. Every so often a war that *must* be fought comes along, and I think this is one of them."

"Yeah, fair enough," I mumble. "But is a nutjob the best man to lead the fight against the bad guys?"

"If not Dr. Oystein, then who?" Burke asks. "You?"

"Hell, no. I'm not a leader."

"Nor am I," Burke says. "It takes a certain breed of person to command. Dr. Oystein is a rarity, a man with the ability to lead but not the desire—he's told me that he's only doing this because it's him or nobody, and I believe him. The alternative is someone who craves power—the likes of Josh Massoglia or Dr. Cerveris. Do you really want to pledge yourself to someone like that?"

"No, but..." I shift uncomfortably. "I didn't like Josh or Dr. Cerveris, but they ran a tight ship."

"Until Mr. Dowling penetrated their defenses," Burke says, then leads me from the Victorian chamber, through the rest of the Dungeon, and out towards the front of the building. When we're in the fresh air, beneath the shadow of the London Eye, he continues.

"This is a chance to start afresh," he says softly. "Whether it was divine retribution or a mess of our own making, the world *has* fallen, the old order *has* crashed and burned. If we can find a way to deal with the zombies, this is an incredible opportunity to begin again and try to improve upon the mistakes of the past.

"If you believe the stories of the Old Testament in the Bible, this isn't the first time this has happened. The Flood wiped the slate clean and people had to start over. Things didn't work out too well that time, but who's to say we can't do better now? The zombies and mutants are clear-cut enemies. Everyone can recognize them as a threat and join against them—Jew, Christian, Muslim, Hindu, white and black, all fighting together, differences set aside.

"If we win this war, power-hungry people will immediately start thinking about how to establish control over the remnants of mankind. They'll look for new foes and threats, and work the survivors up into an agitated state. Hatred and domination are the ways of the past and will in all likelihood be the ways of the future too. Unless Dr. Oystein and his Angels can help us change."

Burke makes a face. "I know I'm being a crazy optimist, but I can't help myself. The best that the old leaders can offer is a return to the status quo. I think, based on what I've seen of him, that Dr. Oystein holds the promise of true redemption. He's what a leader should be—a man who is reluctant to tell others how they should behave and what they should believe."

"I don't know if I agree with you," I say miserably. "I want to, but I can't get over the fact that this is a guy who claims to be in touch with God. It's hard for me to go along with someone like that."

Burke nods. "I understand. I won't try to pressure you, just as Dr. Oystein won't. If you can reconcile yourself to working with us, we'll welcome your support and you can help us take the fight to Mr. Dowling, rescue survivors, work with those who've established compounds beyond the confines of the city, search for a way to suppress the zombies. There's going to be so much to do, so many wars to be waged. We'll need all the help we can get.

"But if you can't trust the doctor, we'll respect your decision. You're free to leave any time you want. I doubt you'll find a more secure home anywhere else in this ruin of a country, but if you need to search for one, you'll depart with our best wishes."

I growl uncertainly. "I want to stay with you, but I'm gonna need more time to think about it."

"That's fine," Burke says. "We're in no rush. Take all the time you want." He turns to leave, then looks back at me with a wicked twinkle in his eyes. "You know what might help?"

"What?" I ask suspiciously.

Burke points to the sky. "You could pray," he says, then skips along with a laugh as I hurl a most unholy curse after him.

THREE

I head back to the training room and find Master Zhang still there, sitting in a corner. He nods for me to enter when he sees me in the doorway. I take up a position opposite him. He's sitting cross-legged on the floor, but I just plop down on my bum and draw my knees up to my chest.

There's a sweet smell in the air. Some kind of flavored tea. It's coming from a pot to the master's right. There's a kettle of water boiling on a small stove to his left.

"I miss the taste of tea more than anything," he says softly, lifting the lid of the pot to stir the contents. "It was one of the great pleasures of my life. I did not realize how important it was to me until I was denied it."

Zhang sniffs the fumes then pours some more water into the pot. He turns off the stove and leaves the kettle to cool. There are some cups stacked behind him. He reaches back slowly, picks up two, passes one to me and sets the other down in front of him.

"Is this a tea ceremony?" I ask.

"You know of such things?" He sounds surprised.

"I saw it on a few travel programs. Looked like a lot of hassle for a simple cup of tea."

"The tea ceremony is an ancient Japanese ritual," Zhang says, pouring a cup of tea for me and one for himself. "It has much more to do with etiquette and tradition than tea. It is a purification process for the soul, a way to honor your guests and bond with them.

"This is not a tea ceremony," he says, picking up his cup and inhaling. "I just enjoy the smell and the memory of the taste."

Zhang sips from the cup, swishes the liquid round his mouth, then picks up a bowl that had been standing next to the cups and spits into it. He passes me the bowl and I follow suit, smelling the fumes, sipping the tea and spitting it out.

"Didn't get much of a kick from it," I note.

"No," he says sadly. "This is a delicate blend. The flavors are subtle and difficult to detect even with an appreciative tongue. With our useless taste buds, we might as well be sipping water."

"Then why bother?" I frown.

"We might not be able to dream," Zhang says, "but we can use our imaginations. With the aid of the scent and the texture of the tea, I can sometimes trick myself into believing that I still taste."

16

He takes another sip, swishes, spits it out and makes a sighing sound. "This is not one of those days."

We take a few more sips, pretending there's a point to this. The smell grows on me after a while, and sets me thinking about something.

"Why do you suppose we can smell when we can't taste?"

I'm not really expecting an answer, but Zhang surprises me.

"It is for practical reasons," he says. "Zombies need to smell, in order to be able to sniff out brains. But since brains are all we eat, we can function without our taste buds."

I scratch my head, thinking it over. "Yeah, that makes sense. I should have figured it out before."

"Yes," Zhang says. "You should have."

I scowl, then laugh. "You're Chinese, aren't you?" I ask, changing the subject.

"Yes."

"But the tea ceremony is Japanese...."

"I have traveled widely," he says. "I like to think of myself as a citizen of the world. Besides, the Chinese introduced tea to Japan, so I feel that I have a natural entitlement to engage in the ceremony."

"What's the situation like in China now?" I ask.

"Not good," he says quietly. "We had the largest population in the world. That means we now have the largest number of zombies. Life is grim everywhere for those who have survived, but it is particularly difficult in China and India."

We finish off the tea in silence. When we're done, Zhang stands and moves to the center of the room, beckoning me to follow. I stand opposite him, ready to be hurled to the floor. But this time he throws a punch at my face.

With a yelp, I knock his hand aside and step back. He follows, throwing another punch. Again I block it and move away from him. Zhang sweeps his leg beneath both of mine and I fall in a heap.

"What the hell!" I snap, rolling away from him.

"You blocked admirably," he says calmly. "And your first defensive step was well judged. Your second, on the other hand..." He tuts.

I stand and dust myself off. "Is this the start of my real training?" I ask.

"No," he says. "The real training started the first time I threw you."

He chops at me and forces me back again. This time I repel four of his attacks before he sweeps my feet from under me.

"You know what I mean," I mutter, rising again. "Are you going to teach me to fight now, to strike and defend myself, the way you teach the others?"

"Yes," he says, and comes forward a third time, lifting his left foot high to kick my chest. I grab the leg and try to twist it. Zhang rolls with the twist, brings his right leg up and kicks the side of my head, knocking me to the ground.

"That was ambitious," he says. "Ambition is good. Caution is better, at least to begin with."

"You're telling me to walk before I try to run?" I ask, getting up again.

"No," he says. "We have no time for walking here. You must learn swiftly and take shortcuts. I do not have time to train you in all the ways of the martial arts. So, when in doubt, go for the simplest solution."

Zhang kicks at me with his left foot again. This time I chop at his ankle then step back out of reach.

"Good," he grunts, and closes in, kicking, punching, chopping, forcing me back, testing my reflexes.

Zhang spars with me for half an hour before telling me to go and rest. "You did well," he says. "We will focus on specific moves next time. This was a useful first workout."

I bow to Master Zhang and turn to leave. But something's niggling me. I stop and face him again. He raises the eyebrow of his bloodshot eye – it must have been bloodshot when he was turned into a zombie, and since we don't heal properly, I'm guessing it will be like that forever – then nods to let me know I can speak.

"Did Dr. Oystein tell you to do this?" I ask. "To step up my training and stop just throwing me about?"

"Why would you think that?" he replies.

"Dr. Oystein told me about his conversations with God."

Zhang's expression doesn't change. He waits for me to continue.

"I think it's a load of nonsense. I'm not sure if I believe in God. Even if I do, I don't think He talks to zombies and asks them to save the world."

"You must be a wise young lady to be able to dismiss the teachings and beliefs of your elders so easily," Zhang says.

"Of course I'm not," I say sourly. "I know my limits. But my nose works as well as yours. I recognize bullshit when I smell it."

"Really?" Zhang smiles thinly. "Did you eat cheese when you were alive?"

I look at him as if he's crazy. "What sort of a question is that?"

"A simple one. I enjoyed cheese very much and tried many varieties over the years. They all tasted good to me, but the smell... Some smelled as good as they tasted. Others stank of old socks, fresh vomit, even, yes, *bullshit*."

"Is this one of those famous Chinese riddles?" I ask when he doesn't continue.

"No," he says. "I am merely pointing out the fact that sometimes one cannot judge by smell alone. Oystein said nothing to me of his meeting with you. I decided to vary your routine because I thought the time was right. I will be doing the same with Rage when he next comes to me. There is nothing more to it than that, no matter what your nose might tell you."

"Fair enough," I grunt.

"You believe me?" he asks.

"Yeah."

"Then why don't you believe Oystein?"

"Because you're not telling me that you can talk with God." I pause. "You're not, are you?"

21

Zhang shakes his head. "I do not believe in God. Or reincarnation. Or any kind of supernatural realm." He makes a small sighing sound, looking his age for once—he can only have been in his early twenties when he was turned into a zombie. "My lack of faith was a source of grave concern for my parents."

"Then what the hell are you doing here?" I growl.

He shrugs. "I believe in the doctor. He rescued me years ago. I was living in a small village but had moved there from a large city. I had been vaccinated against the zombie gene. Oystein kept track of me, the way he tried to keep track of all his children—and that is how he thinks of us.

"When there was an outbreak of zombies in my village, troops moved in to contain it. We were sealed off from the world and those who had been infected were executed. Oystein made sure that I was not killed. He had me isolated and fed. My guardians were issued with strict instructions not to harm me.

"I took almost five months to revitalize. Most people would have given up on me. Not Oystein. He hates abandoning any of us."

"But it's got to be a problem for you," I mutter. "How can you believe in him if you don't believe he really speaks with God?"

"It is not an issue," Zhang insists. "He has never asked me to accept his beliefs. He has only asked me to fight, which is all he is asking of you too."

Zhang returns to his cups and bowls and begins to tidy them away. "It is very straightforward in my view," he says. "A war to decide the future of this planet is being fought. We must choose sides or pretend it is not happening. Assuming you do not go down the road of blind ignorance, and are not on the side of evil, you must back Oystein, regardless of whatever flaws you perceive in him, or look for another leader to support."

"Do you think there are others out there?"

"I am sure there are. But they will have flaws too. You must ask yourself which is worse—a leader firmly rooted in reality who thirsts for power and control, or a truly good-hearted man who might be a touch delusional.

"I do not think that God exists," Zhang says, heading for the door. "But there are certainly godly people on this planet, and I am honored that one of them has deemed me worthy of his friendship and support. You should be too, as I doubt there are many pure people in this world who would see goodness within *you*." He looks at me with a probing expression. "Do you even see it within yourself?"

I think of the bad things I have done. Of my racist past. Of Tyler Bayor.

And I can't say a word.

"I will see you tomorrow for training," Zhang says softly, and shuts the door with a heel, leaving me even more confused and unsure than I was when I came in.

FOUR

I head back to my room, taking my time, creeping through the deserted corridors of County Hall, thinking about all that I've been told. As I'm passing one of the building's many chambers, I hear a strange moaning noise. I slow down and the noise comes again. It sounds like someone in pain. Worried, I open the door. The room is pitch-black.

"Hello?" I call out nervously, wary of a trap.

"Who's that?" a girl snaps.

"B," I reply, relaxing now that I've placed the voice.

There's a pause. Then the girl says, "Come in and close the door."

Shutting the door behind me, I shuffle forward into darkness. I'm about to ask for directions when a dim light is switched on. I spot the twins, Awnya and Cian, in a corner. Awnya is sitting against a wall. Cian is lying on the floor, his head buried in his sister's lap. He's trembling and moaning into his hands, which are covering his face. Awnya is stroking the back of her brother's head with one hand, holding a small flashlight with the other.

I cross the room and squat beside Awnya. "What's going on?" I whisper as Cian makes a low-pitched weeping noise, his body shaking violently. "Is he sick?"

"Only sick of this world," Awnya says quietly. She looks at me with a pained expression. "We often come to a quiet place like this. We feel so lonely and we've seen so many horrors… Sometimes it gets too much for us and we have to break down and cry."

"Zombies can't cry," I remind her.

"Not the normal way," she agrees, "but we can cry in our own fashion." She strokes Cian's head again. "We take it in turns to comfort one another. We can't both break down at the same time or we might never recover. One of us always looks out for the other."

Cian starts to gibber nonsense sentences, then he curses and whimpers. Awnya lays down her flashlight, massages his shoulders with both hands and sings to him, an old ballad that I vaguely recognize. It should be laughable but it's strangely touching.

"Do you want me to leave?" I whisper between verses.

"Not unless you feel awkward," Awnya says, and carries on singing.

I lay my head against the wall and listen to the song. I'd like to close my eyes but I can't. Instead I study the shadows thrown across the room by the flashlight. There are cobwebs running along the top of the skirting board opposite us. The world has gone to hell, but life goes on as usual for these spiders. They know nothing of zombies, mutants, God. They just spin their webs and wait for dinner. Lucky sods.

Cian eventually stops sniveling and sits up. He rubs his cheeks and smiles shakily at me, embarrassed but not mortified.

"We're lucky," Awnya says, brushing Cian's blond hair out of his eyes. "We have each other. I don't know how the rest of you cope."

I shrug. "You learn to deal with it."

"It's because we're the youngest," Cian mutters. "Dr. Oystein says that a year or two makes a big difference. He says we can go to him anytime we want, for comfort or anything else, but he thinks it's better if we can support ourselves."

"This is a hard world for the weak," Awnya notes.

"We're not *weak*," Cian snaps.

Awnya rolls her eyes, then squints at me. "Did Dr. Oystein tell you everything?"

"Yeah."

"It's brilliant, isn't it?" Cian says. "Being on the side of God and all."

"I think it's scary," Awnya murmurs.

"That's because you're a girl. Girls are soft," Cian sniffs, apparently forgetting that moments earlier he was whining like a baby. "I'm not afraid of the Devil, Mr. Dowling or anyone else."

"Of course you are," Awnya says. "We all are. And we're right to be afraid, aren't we, B? You met the clown. He's as scary as Dr. Oystein says, isn't he?"

I nod slowly. "He's a terrifying bugger, there's no doubt about that. But as for him working for the Devil, don't make me laugh."

"What do you mean?" Awnya asks.

"You don't really believe that, do you, about God and the Devil?"

"Of course we do," Cian says stiffly. "Dr. Oystein told us."

"And you buy everything he says?" I sneer.

"Yes, actually," Awnya growls, pushing herself away from me.

"Dr. Oystein saved us," Cian says.

"He gave us a home," Awnya says.

"He's a saint," Cian says.

"Our only hope for the future," Awnya says.

"Yeah, yeah," I rumble. "He's doing a fantastic job and he's a first-rate geezer, but that doesn't change the fact that he's crazy. If God is real, He doesn't get involved in our affairs. This is all about what our stupid scientists and armies have done to the world, not about a war between God and Satan."

"Hmm," Awnya says, pretending to think hard. "Who should I trust? A genius who's been working for decades to try to save mankind, or a girl with a chip on her shoulder?"

"What chip?" I grunt.

29

"I don't know," Awnya says. "But you must have one, otherwise why are you saying nasty things about Dr. Oystein? You've only been here five minutes, yet you're telling us we're stupid, that we should listen to you instead of the man who loves and protects us."

"I'm just saying it's madness," I whisper.

"Dr. Oystein's maybe the only person in this world who *isn't* mad," Cian huffs. "God spoke to him, touched him, changed him. He's the best of us all."

"You really believe that?"

"Yes," Cian says.

"Absolutely," Awnya says.

"One hundred percent," Cian adds, in case there's any doubt.

"Fine," I shrug, and get to my feet. "I wish I could believe it too. I'm not trying to stir things up. I just can't see it. I want to but I can't."

"Then you're in an even worse state than us," Awnya says, and there's genuine sympathy in her tone.

"Yeah," I say hollowly. "I guess I am."

I start for the door but Awnya stops me. "B?" I look back at her questioningly. "If it's any comfort, we're jealous of you."

"Why?" I frown.

"Dr. Oystein and Master Zhang chose you to fight," she says.

"They didn't pick us," Cian says glumly.

"Dr. Oystein loves us all," Awnya says, "but even though I'm sure he'd deny it, he's got to love his warriors more than the likes of

30

Cian and me. You're the ones who are going to defeat Mr. Dowling and save the world."

"We're just the guys who find things for the rest of you," Cian says.

"If we could swap places with you, we would," Awnya says.

I scratch my head while I think that over. "You two are a couple of freaks," I finally mumble. We all laugh—they know I meant it in a nice way. Cian and Awnya wave politely at me. I flip them a friendly finger then let myself out.

FIVE

All of my roommates are present when I get to my bedroom, including Rage, who's studying Ashtat's model of the Houses of Parliament.

"It's all matchsticks?" he's asking.

"Yes," Ashtat says.

"There isn't a ready-made frame underneath that you've stuck them onto?"

"No, it is all my own work."

"Cool."

Ashtat smiles sappily and tugs shyly at her white headscarf.

"You want to be careful," I call to her, "or he'll burn the bugger down."

Rage grins. "Don't say such nasty things about me, Becky. I want to make a good impression on my new friends."

"You don't have any friends here," I snort.

"Isn't that for us to decide?" Ashtat snaps.

"She's got a point," Carl says. "We know you don't like this guy, but that doesn't mean the rest of us have to hate him."

"Yeah," Shane grunts. "He seems all right to me."

"He's a killer," I growl. "I saw him murder a man."

"She's got me dead to rights," Rage says chirpily as the others stare at him. "I can't deny it. Guilty as charged, officer."

Rage swaggers over to his bed and sits on it, testing the springs.

"What Miss Smith *might* have failed to mention," he adds, "was that I'd been kept captive and denied brains for several days, which meant I was close to reverting and becoming a mindless revived. The man I killed had imprisoned and starved me. In my eyes that made him fair game."

"The rest of us had been starved too," I snarl. "We didn't turn into killers."

"As I recall, you were quite keen to tuck into Dr. Cerveris's brain once I'd cut open his skull," Rage notes. "If I hadn't stopped you, you'd have torn in like a pig at feeding time."

"Maybe," I concede. "But I didn't kill him. You were the only one of us who killed."

"Really?" Rage starts looking around as if searching for something. He even bends and peers under the bed. "Where's Mark?" he finally asks.

"Bastard," I sneer.

"Reilly told me what happened," Rage chuckles. "Your lot found out Mark was alive and you tore the poor sod apart. True or false?"

"The others did. Not me."

"You abstained?"

"Yeah."

"Then you have my respect," Rage says quietly, his smile fading. "You were able to control yourself. You're a better person than I am. Better than any of the zom heads were. But will you look down your nose at those of us who are made of weaker material?"

I stare at Rage uncomfortably. I didn't expect the argument to go like this. He was supposed to fight his corner, not praise me and make me feel bad for insulting him.

"I'm not proud of what I did in that hellhole," Rage says. "But I was in bad shape. I needed brains. If it hadn't been Dr. Cerveris, if it had been someone good and decent, would I have killed them anyway? I like to think not, but I can't say for sure."

I gulp – old habits die hard – and try to think of something to say, but I can't.

"All this honesty," Rage says, grinning again. "I never knew how invigorating it would make me feel to tell the truth all the time. You should try it, Becky. A bit of honesty's good for the soul."

"I can be as honest as anyone," I shout. "I hate your guts and always will, no matter what you say or do. How honest is that?"

"Good enough for me," Rage laughs, cocking his head swiftly to the side, the closest any of us living dead can get to a wink.

I stomp to my bed, throw myself down and glare at the ceiling. A few minutes later, Carl comes and sits beside me. He's changed his clothes again, choosing an old-fashioned suit that looks plain wrong on a guy his age. He's brushed his dark hair back too, gelling it flat the way businessmen used to in old movies that I sometimes watched with my dad on a lazy Sunday. All he needs is a bowler hat and a fancy umbrella and he could be a fresh-faced banker from fifty or sixty years ago.

"How are you feeling?" he asks softly.

"Sick to my stomach at having to share a room with *him*," I snap.

"I meant about the rest of it, what Dr. Oystein told you."

I prop myself on one elbow and squint at Carl, who looks a bit sheepish.

"It can be hard to take it all in when he first tells you," Carl continues. "I was in shock for a few days. There's so much to think about and process."

"You don't believe either," I whisper. "You think he's mad."

"Who's that?" Rage pipes up. "The doc? You can bet your sorry excuse for a life that he is. Mad as a hatter."

"You shouldn't say things like that," Shane barks.

"Why not?" Rage shrugs. "It's what I think, how I feel. The doc won't mind. He has bigger things to worry about than whether or not the likes of us think he's the Messiah or a howling maniac." He looks around at everyone. "Come on, how many of you really believe that he speaks with God?"

36

Ashtat and Shane stick up their hands immediately. Jakob starts to raise his, wincing at the pain as he lifts his thin, skeletal arm, but then he stops and shakes his head. "I don't know," he croaks.

Carl keeps his hands on his knees. He looks troubled.

"Three against three," Rage beams. "Sounds about right to me. This world has always split down the middle when it comes to gurus. One man's prophet is another man's crackpot."

"The difference here," I mutter, "is that those who doubt don't usually throw themselves behind the lunatics."

"Of course they do," Rage says. "People pick their religion for all sorts of selfish, unspiritual reasons. We don't choose our holy men just because we think they'll sort us out when we die and our souls move on—we like to get some benefit from them in this life too."

"I can see now why B doesn't like you," Carl sniffs. "You're a real cynic."

"It's my best quality," Rage smirks. "But you're the same. Why are you trailing around after the doc if you don't believe he speaks with God? No need to answer. I know already. He's good for you. He set you up in this swanky spot, provides you with brains, trains you to fight. You'd have to be crazy to walk away from a cushy number like this. If the only downside of that is having to swallow his *I am the Right Hand of God* rubbish, well, that's an easy enough sacrifice to make. Am I right or am I right?"

"You think you're clever, don't you?" Carl growls.

"I do, actually, yeah," Rage chuckles, then gets up and walks

over to the foot of my bed. He stares down at me as I glare up at him. "What's your problem?" Rage asks, and he sounds genuinely curious. "You've a face like a slapped arse. Why can't you just take the doc's out-there beliefs with a grain of salt and go along for the ride like everyone else?"

"It's not that simple," I mumble.

"Of course it is," Rage says. "All you have to do is hold your tongue when the doc's warbling on about heavenly missions. How hard can that be? In fact I bet he doesn't mention it that often. Am I right, Clay?"

Carl nods. "He's barely mentioned religion to me since that first time. In fact he even apologizes on the rare occasions when he name-drops God, since he knows that makes some people feel uncomfortable."

"See?" Rage beams. "Simple, like I told you."

"It's not!" I shout, pushing Carl away and getting to my feet. I think about picking a fight with Rage but I don't. And it's not just because I know he'd wipe the floor with me. He's trying to help. He deserves an answer, not an angry retort.

"It's because of my dad," I say sadly, sinking back onto my bed. "He wasn't a nice guy. He used to beat me and my mum, and he was a racist. He made me do something even worse than what Rage and the other zom heads did underground..."

I spill my guts, telling them everything, about Dad, how he campaigned to keep England white, the way he pressured me to copy his lead, how I went along with him for the sake of a quiet life. I end with what happened to Tyler Bayor, Dad screaming at me to throw him to the zombies, obeying because it was what I'd become accustomed to.

I choke up towards the end. I'd cry if I could, but of course the tears aren't there and never will be again. Still, my chest heaves and my voice shakes. I even let rip with a few involuntary moans, like Cian a while earlier.

There's a long silence when I finish. Everyone's looking at me, but I don't glance up to check whether they're staring with sympathy or loathing.

"I knew my dad for what he was," I moan. "A nasty sod, a bully, a manipulator. In the end, a monster. But I loved him anyway. I still do. If he walked in now, I'd hug him and tell him how much I've missed him, and it would be true. He was my father, whatever his faults."

I get up and wander across the room to the model of the Houses of Parliament that Ashtat has been working on. I stare at it, gathering my thoughts.

"People complained about politicians in the old days, called them self-serving, greedy, power-hungry gits. But hardly anyone tried to change the system. They were our elected leaders and we felt like we had to go along with them because there was no other way.

"I did that with my dad and it was wrong, just as people were wrong to put up with the political creeps. There's *always* another way. If it's not clear-cut, we have to work hard to find it. We shouldn't

40

trudge along, putting our faith in people who don't deserve it, accepting things because we're afraid of what will happen if we break ranks and try to build something better.

"Dad was a good man in certain ways. He was loyal to his friends. I don't think he ever cheated on Mum. He was brave—he risked his life to try to save me when the zombies attacked. But he thought that whites were superior to other races. It was a huge flaw in him. I could see it, but I put up with it because I didn't dare confront him."

I turn away from the model and face the others. "Dr. Oystein's like my dad. A good man in many ways, but too sure of himself and the way the world should be ordered. I can't believe that God spoke to him. That doesn't seem to be an issue for Rage and Carl, but it is for me. Because I've seen what happens when you put your trust in people like that. They break your heart." I tug at the material of my T-shirt and grimace. "Some of the buggers even rip it from your chest."

Then I go and lie down and stare at the ceiling and don't say anything else for the rest of the night.

SIX

I train hard for the next week. Now that Master Zhang has started practicing proper moves with me, I learn new things every day. It's a real mix—karate, judo, boxing. We also focus a lot on fighting with knives, steel bars, hammers, screwdrivers, things like that.

"This is all about practical application," he tells me. "Apart from some knives, we will not send you out armed. You will fight mostly with your hands, but if you ever need a weapon, you must know how to make use of whatever you can find."

I ask him why we don't use guns. "The zombies don't have any. Surely we could just go out with rifles and mow them down."

"There would be no honor in that," he replies.

"But isn't this all about winning?" I press.

"Not at any cost," he says. "Oystein is adamant about that. If we are to build a better world, we cannot do so by relying on the barbaric ways of the past."

"Reilly has a taser," I note.

"Reilly is human," Zhang says calmly. "We are not. We have a choice—we can be less than we were or we can try to be more."

"It would be a lot easier if we had guns," I mutter.

"The easy way is not always the better way," he says. "If we wish to rise above our foul situation, we must work harder to be honorable in death than we ever had to in life."

Zhang shows me how to most effectively sharpen the bones sticking out of my fingers and toes. He says they're our best weapons and he teaches me how to incorporate them into the moves, how to dig and slice and gouge.

He also trains me to file my teeth in a different way. "You never know when you might have to rip out someone's throat or chew through to their brain in a hurry."

"Is there honor in biting open a person's throat?" I ask innocently.

"Less of your back talk," he growls, but I know he's smirking inside. We get along all right. We're similar in many ways. Tough nuts.

I don't discuss Dr. Oystein with the other Angels. In fact I don't talk to them much at all. I've been brooding ever since that day in the aquarium. No matter which way I look at it, I can't accept what the doc told me. And being unable to accept that he's on a mission from God, I find it hard to accept anything else about him, his offer of refuge or a role in the war he's waging. Rage and Carl are able to sweep their misgivings under the carpet. I can't.

Rage is fitting in better than me. He's in his element, training hard with Master Zhang, messing about with our roommates, getting to know other Angels. He's taken to this with ease.

That pisses me off. I was sure that Rage would be the outcast here, the one that the others would be wary of. I was almost looking forward to the day when he betrayed us, so I could say, "Told you so!" But, as things stand, I'm the one who doesn't belong, who's falling adrift a little further every day. It's not that the others aren't trying to be nice to me. They are. But I see them as stooges who are playing along with Dr. Oystein for all the wrong reasons, so I feel awkward around them and keep pushing them away.

The worst thing is, there's no one for me to confide in. I've seen Dr. Oystein a few times over the week, in corridors, the dining room and gym. He's always smiled at me, made small talk a few times. I'm sure he'd be happy to discuss my concerns if I approached him, but what could I say? "Sorry, doc, I think you're crazy and dangerous. Other than that you're OK."

Mr. Burke is the only person I'd feel comfortable chatting about this with, but he's gone off again on a mission, to infiltrate another complex like the one where I was held captive, or to spy on Mr. Dowling, or…

Actually, I don't know what Burke, Dr. Oystein and the others get up to. There hasn't been much talk of how we're supposed to take the fight to Mr. Dowling and his mutants. Things seem to operate on a need-to-know basis around here. Or maybe it's on an *if-we-can-trust-her* basis. Perhaps they're withholding information from me because they sense that I'm not fully committed.

I suppose that's logical. You don't want to share all your secrets with someone who might walk out the door at any given moment. In their position I wouldn't be too forthcoming with someone like me either. Still, that doesn't make life any easier, just increases my belief that it's me against the rest of them. Roll on, full-blown paranoia!

"Oh, this is ridiculous," I snap, and push myself away from the table.

I'm in the dining room, having just tucked into a bowl of Ciara's latest batch of cranial stew. The others are still chewing. They stare at me uncertainly, surprised by my outburst.

"What's wrong?" Ciara asks, having stayed to chat with Reilly, who's munching a hamburger that I'd give my left ear to be able to taste. "Is it too hot? Too cold? Lumpy?"

"I wasn't talking about the food." I force a smile, not wanting to offend the sweet, fashionably dressed dinner lady. "The food's great. Honest. I just... I can't deal with this anymore. I've got to get some air. I'm going for a walk. I'll be back later."

I storm away. I don't know why things should have come to a

head here, now, but they have. Something inside me snapped when I was sitting at the table, thinking about Dr. Oystein and his claim to have a link to a higher power, and how everyone is happy to go along with whatever the doc says. I've been playing the good little girl, saying nothing, but I can't do it anymore.

I'm tramping down a corridor, not sure where I'm going or what my plans are, when someone rushes up behind me. Before I can react, arms snake across my stomach and grab me. I'm hauled into the air and twirled round. I catch a glimpse of Rage's face as I'm whirling.

"Let me go!" I shout.

"Your wish is my command," he says, and instantly releases me.

I stagger across the floor, slam into a wall and fall. My head is spinning badly. I lean forward and dry heave. There are white flashes in front of my eyes.

"Are you all right?" Rage asks.

"No," I gasp, then sit back against the wall and wait for my head to clear. When it finally does and the heaving stops, I glare at him. "What did you do that for?"

"Just trying to cheer you up. Did you get dizzy?"

"What does it look like, numbnuts?"

"Did that used to happen when you were spun around in the past?" he asks.

"Yeah. Not as bad as this, but my ears were never the best. They used to pop like mad when I flew. If I went on a spinning ride at a carnival, I'd have a headache for hours."

"Oh. I thought it might be something to do with being dead. I was worried for a minute."

"No need to be," I snarl, getting to my feet. "You can still go on merry-go-rounds anytime you like."

"I preferred you when you were suffering," Rage sniffs, and reaches out to grab me again.

"You'll lose both hands if you try it," I snap, then squint at him. "Why the hell are you trying to cheer me up anyway? What does it matter to you how I feel?"

"It doesn't," he says. "But the others thought someone should come after you. They were concerned, thought you might do something stupid, maybe off yourself. I figured I'd look like a caring, sensitive guy if I volunteered to help you, especially as they all know that you hate me. So here I am."

"You're too sweet for this world," I jeer. "Head on back to those muppets and tell them I'm fine."

"Not yet," Rage says. "It's too soon. It wouldn't look like I'd tried very hard. I'll tag along with you for a while."

"What if I don't want you to?"

"Tough." He flashes me a grin. "If you do want to off yourself, I know a place where you can get some great power drills. I'll even help you choose the best bit for it. I'd love to see someone drill through their own skull."

"There's the Rage I know and loathe," I chuckle.

"*Honest Rage*," he smirks. "That's how I define myself these days. Telling the truth is what I'm all about."

"It must be a nice change," I sneer.

"It is." There's a long silence while we eye each other. "But seriously," Rage says, breaking it, "if you *do* want me to recommend a good drill..."

SEVEN

We exit County Hall and walk to the corner of the building. We can see part of Waterloo Station from here, and the London Eye.

"Have you been back into the station since Zhang tested us?" Rage asks.

I look at him oddly. "No. Why the hell would I?"

"I have," he says. "I've gone in there with a rucksack seeded with brains, done the run through the zombies again, trying to improve my time."

"Why?" I frown.

"I want to be top dog. You've got to push yourself if you want to get ahead."

"You'd better be careful," I say drily, "or you'll wear yourself out."

"Nah," Rage grins. "It's not just all about the training. I make time for fun stuff too. For instance, I walked up to the IMAX theater the other day. Wanted to see if I could screen a film."

"Could you?" I ask.

"Wasn't able to try. The place was packed with zombies. I forced my way through to the projectionist's booth, but the buggers had beaten me to it. Some of them had made it their home and it was a mess, equipment smashed to pieces. A shame. I was hoping to screen *Night of the Living Dead* there."

It's hard to tell if he's joking or not.

"The noise would have been awful anyway," I note. "The IMAX had the best sound system in London, great for a living person with normal hearing, but with ears like ours it would have been deafening."

"Yeah," Rage says. "But fun. The reviveds would have hated it. They'd have howled like wolves." He stretches, looks at the sky and grimaces. It's a cloudy day but still way too bright for the likes of us. "Where were you headed before I stopped you?"

"Nowhere."

"Really? You were marching like a girl with a purpose."

"I just wanted to get away."

Rage scratches an armpit and grunts. Must be force of habit— we don't sweat, so he can't have itchy pits.

"It's boring here, isn't it?" he says. "That's why I keep looking for

52

things to do. I hate the silence. A city should be buzzing, not quiet like this. It's like the God-awful countryside these days."

"Nothing wrong with the countryside," I sniff. "I used to enjoy days out."

"No, you didn't," Rage argues. "It was hell out there, nothing but fields, trees and Mother bloody Nature. If people loved that so much, they wouldn't have built cities and moved to them. The countryside's boring and so's London now."

He turns in a circle, looking for something to amuse himself. He pauses when he spots the London Eye, then nods at me. "Come on."

"I'm not going on the Eye. I've been up a few times since I moved into County Hall. It always leaves me feeling down, seeing how much of the city has been ruined."

"Just follow me," he insists.

At the Eye, instead of hopping aboard one of the pods, he heads for the control booth. There's always an Angel on watch in a pod, as well as one in the booth to monitor the big wheel. Today the person on duty is Ivor, a guy I know pretty well, although I wouldn't claim to be a close friend. I first ran into him when he was on a mission with his team, and we've had a few conversations since then, when our paths have crossed.

Ivor has brought a load of locks with him, and is fiddling with them to while away the time. He's able to pick just about any lock.

I'd love to be able to do that, but although I've tried a few times, I'm not a natural.

"Don't you ever stop practicing?" Rage shouts, startling Ivor, who was focused on the locks and didn't see us approach. He almost drops the lock that he's working on, but catches it just in time.

"It's good to keep your hand in," Ivor says, smiling at us. "My fingers are like a lock—they get rusty if I don't keep using them."

Ivor spends a few minutes showing us how to pick the lock. He makes it look so easy, but I get nowhere with it. Rage doesn't even try.

"These fingers weren't made for work like that," he says, giving them a wiggle.

"They're like sausages," I laugh.

"Yeah," he says. "Perfect for smashing, not picking."

We chat with Ivor for a while, then Rage asks if he can stop the Eye.

"Stop it?" Ivor frowns.

"Just for ten or fifteen minutes. You don't mind, do you?"

"I'm not supposed to," Ivor says. "Dr. Oystein likes us to keep it going all the time."

"I know. But we'll pretend that someone in a wheelchair was boarding and they got stuck."

Ivor laughs. Rage works on him a bit more and finally he agrees to the odd request.

"But no more than a quarter of an hour," he insists. "And if the doc or Master Zhang asks, I'll tell them it was for you."

"Cheers," Rage says, hurrying out of the booth.

"What are you up to?" I ask suspiciously as I follow him.

"You'll see in a sec," he promises, and trots to the nearest pod.

There are small handles running around the pod. Rage grabs hold and climbs quickly until he's standing on the roof. I still don't know what he's planning, but I'm curious, so I climb up after him.

"They must be the biggest spokes in the world," Rage says, staring at the mesh of links above us. "Imagine if you had another wheel the size of this and you could make a bike out of them."

"You're crazy," I laugh.

"Yeah," he grins, then jumps and grabs hold of one of the bars. He pulls himself up then slides across until he's hugging the rim of the wheel. "Race you."

"What?"

"Race you," he beams. "Come on, up you get."

I stare at him uncertainly.

"Are you chicken?" he growls.

"Sod you," I snap. "I just don't know what you're talking about."

"A race," he says. "Along the inside of the rim, all the way to the top."

I frown, then study the metal rim. I follow it with my gaze as it curves outwards and upwards, before arcing back in on itself past the halfway mark and coming full circle at the top.

"You *are* bloody crazy!" I gasp, seeing now what he wants to do.

"I might be crazy but I'm no coward," Rage chuckles. "Come on, I dare you—a race. We're stronger than we were. We've got these neat bones sticking out of our fingers and toes to help us grip. I'm sure we can do it."

"Even if we could, why the hell would we want to?"

"Now who's the crazy one?" he jeers. "I'm challenging you to a race up the London Eye. Nobody could have done that in the past, not without equipment. How cool will it be to be the first pair in the world to free-climb this baby?"

"It's impossible," I mumble. "If we made it past the halfway point, we'd have to hang upside down." I point to the bar running up the center of the Eye, linking the two rims of the wheel. Smaller bars from the rims connect with it at regular intervals. We could use them for support. "What about that way? It would be safer and easier."

"This isn't about safe and easy," Rage says. "I think we'll be all right even if we fall – we're hard to kill – but if not, what of it? We've all got to go eventually. How would you prefer to leave this world— as a decaying, decrepit old fart, or trying to climb the London Eye in your prime?"

"Dr. Oystein won't like it if a couple of his precious Angels risk their lives on something this pointless," I murmur with a wicked smirk.

"I don't think either one of us is that bothered about keeping Dr. Oystein happy," Rage snorts. "Last one up's a rotten zombie!"

And off he shoots.

For a few seconds I shake my head and tut loudly. Then, with a whoop, I leap, grab hold of a bar, pull myself up, steady myself on the rim and off I tear.

EIGHT

This is crazy. I know that even before I start. But hell, there's no denying it's fun! I haven't had an adrenaline rush like this since I returned to consciousness. Well, OK, it's not an actual adrenaline rush, since I doubt my body produces that anymore. But it damn sure feels like it.

The rim of the wheel is thicker than I expected. A cable runs along the inside, good for gripping, but on the outside it's pure steel, which isn't so accommodating.

At first it's easy. I scuttle along, no problem with my toughened flesh and bones. I laugh with delight, not bothered by the sunlight or what might happen to me if I fall, the gloom of the last week forgotten, focusing on nothing except my ascent.

Then it starts to get tricky. The higher I climb, the more gravity drags at me. From the ground the incline didn't look too steep, but when you're up here and following it, you get a fresh perspective. From about the quarter mark it's like climbing at ninety degrees. I start to slip and sway in the breeze, which seems much stronger than it did a few minutes ago.

I struggle on, teeth gritted, refusing to look at the ground. Cuts open on both hands as the steel and cable slice into them when I slip. Thankfully my blood doesn't flow as swiftly as it once did – it just seeps out slowly – or I'd have to stop. As it is, I can push on, pausing every so often to wipe the congealed blood from my palms.

I'm almost halfway up the wheel when I lose my grip completely. I fall with a cry that's cut short when I slam into one of the support poles that connects with the central bar. I cling on desperately as my legs swing freely beneath me. I hear Rage whooping with glee—he must have paused at the perfect time to catch my big slip. I'd love to shoot him the finger but I don't dare loosen my grip.

If I was human, I'd be done for. The wind would have been knocked from my sails, my muscles would be aching from the climb. Not being a Hollywood movie star, I doubt I'd be able to pull myself to safety. It would be the long drop for me.

But being dead has its advantages. I don't breathe, and my body isn't as confined by the laws of physics as it used to be. After dangling for a while, I haul myself up until I'm hanging across the bar.

I wipe my hands dry, steady myself, grip the rim and start climbing again.

I'm just past the halfway mark when Rage shouts to me. "Oi! Smith!" His voice is tinny, coming from so far away, but the wind carries it and my supersharp ears pick it up.

I take a firm hold and look across to where he's hanging opposite me. My eyes are less effective than my ears, so he's only a vague blob in the distance. "What?" I roar.

"What are we gonna do now?" he yells. "It would be easier if we shifted to the outside of the rim. If we stick to the inside, we'll be hanging upside down the rest of the way."

I'd been thinking about that myself. I was going to suggest we move to the other side, so we could crawl on top of the rim instead of dangle from its underside. But now that he's getting cold feet, I don't want to ease up. He was the dope who suggested this crazy challenge. I want to make him go through with it, even though that means me suffering as well.

"If you want to back down, let me know," I roar cheerfully. "I won't tell anyone you chickened out. Well, except for everyone we know."

"Screw you!" he bellows. "I'm game if you are."

"Then what are you waiting for?" I laugh, and start climbing again.

It soon becomes clear that we really *are* mad to attempt this. As hard as it was before, it's ten times more difficult now. I'm hanging from the rim like a squirrel, but squirrels have tails, padded paws and the benefit of countless generations of instinct to draw upon. Humans were never meant to climb like this, not even undead buggers like me.

The hardest parts are where the bars to the inner circle connect. The rim bulges out in those spots and I have to ease around the protuberances. That was easy on the lower sections, but not when I'm hanging upside down and every muscle in my arms is stretched to a snapping point.

I keep my feet hooked over the rim for as much of the climb as I can, dragging them along, feeling the steel and cable slice deeply into my flesh. Pain doesn't hit you as much as it used to when you're a zombie, but we're not immune to it and I'm starting to really sting. I haven't felt this rough since I staggered away from Trafalgar Square after my last encounter with Mr. Dowling.

My feet keep slipping. Eventually, when I move into the last quarter of the climb, I unhook them and hang at full stretch, supported solely by my hands. I was good on the monkey bars in playgrounds when I was a kid. I could swing across as often as I pleased, laughing at the others who couldn't match me. Time to find out if I still have the old magic.

I inch forward, moving my hands one at a time, concentrating as I never have before. I don't want to slip, and it's got nothing to do with the threat of smashing my skull open or the possibility that Rage will beat me to the top. I need to prove to myself that I can do this. As ludicrous as it is, this has become important to me. I figure if I can do this, I can attempt just about anything. Maybe this is what I need to clear my head and haul me out of the miserable, indecisive pit that I've been rotting in this past week.

It feels like the climb is never going to end. I want to shut my eyes but I can't. I want to take the strain from my arms but I can't. I want to rest for a while but... You get the picture.

I spy Rage across from me. He hasn't made it as far as I have. He's struggling. He's stronger than me but a hell of a lot heavier too. In a situation like this, where weight comes into play, it's good to be a slim snip of a girl.

I get a second wind (relatively speaking) when I see that I'm doing better than Rage. With something between a triumphant shout and a despondent groan, I force myself on, finding fresh strength somewhere deep inside me, ignoring the pain, physics, gravity, the whole damn lot.

Finally, when I'm sure I can't go any farther, I reach the highest point. I hang there for several long seconds, staring down at my feet and the drop beneath. I feel strangely peaceful. The pain in my arms seems to fade. If I fell right now and split my head open on a spoke, I could go happy into the great beyond.

But this isn't a day for bidding my final farewell to the world. With a determined moan, I pull myself up, hook a leg over the rim, pause to let my arms recover, then search for the handles on the uppermost pod. Finding them, I haul myself up, almost scurrying compared to the slow pace of my previous progress, and moments later, I'm lying on top of the pod, staring at the clouds in the sky, a BIG smile on my face, waiting for the slow, shamed Rage to join me.

Bloody *yes*, mate!

NINE

Rage crawls onto the roof of the pod about a minute later. He's not huffing or puffing – with our redundant lungs we don't do that anymore – but his limbs are shaking, especially his arms, the same way mine are.

"Sod me!" he gasps, collapsing onto his back and covering his eyes with a weary, trembling arm.

"No thanks," I smirk, then dig him in the ribs with my knuckles. "Who's the queen of the castle and who's a dirty rascal?"

"Get stuffed," he barks.

"Come on, you set the challenge. Don't be a sore loser, just tell me who's the queen and –"

"Enough already," he growls. "You beat me fair and square. Happy?"

"Ecstatic," I beam.

"I don't know how I made it," Rage mutters. "Those last few meters were hell. I just wanted to drop and end the agony."

"You're too big for climbing," I chuckle. "Size matters but sometimes it's better to be small."

"Yeah," he says. "I guess."

We lie there a while longer, relaxing, ignoring the glare of the daylight and the itching it causes. Then the Eye starts slowly revolving again. Ivor either saw us make it to the top or else he decided enough was enough.

I get to my feet to have a good look around. It's hard to see clearly without sunglasses to protect my eyes, but I force myself to turn and peer. Everything's blurred to begin with, but things start to swim into focus (well, as much as they're ever going to) as my eyes slowly adjust.

Rage stands up beside me. He doesn't bother with the sights, just rolls his arms around, working out the kinks and stretching his muscles.

"I bet we'll ache like hell later," I note. "We might even have to go back into the Groove Tubes."

"Dr. Oystein won't let us," Rage says. "He'll make us endure the pain. The Groove Tubes are for Angels who really need them, who get injured in the line of duty, not for thrill seekers like us."

"Oh well," I smile, "I don't care. It was worth it. I never thought I could have done something this amazing. You're still a murderous git, but you made a good call."

"That's what I'm all about," Rage says smugly. "Making good

calls and helping people realize their ambitions. The Good Samaritan had nothing on me."

"He was bit more modest though."

"Screw modesty," Rage sniffs, then takes a step closer to me. "Now, speaking of making good calls, here's another. B?"

I was looking off in the direction of Vauxhall, trying to see if there were any signs of life over there. When Rage calls my name, I turn to face him. My back's to the river.

"Enjoy your flight," Rage says.

And he pushes me off.

My arms flail. I open my mouth to scream. Gravity grabs hold. I fall from the pod and plummet towards the river like a stone.

TEN

I hit the water hard. It feels like slamming into concrete. The lights temporarily blink out inside my head and everything goes dark.

When consciousness flickers on again, I think for a few seconds that I'm properly dead, adrift in a realm of ghosts. There are sinuous shadows all around, encircling and breaking over me. I assume that my brain was terminally damaged in the fall. I turn slowly, at peace, glad in a way to be done with life and all semblance of it. I spot a glimmering zone overhead—the legendary ball of light that summons the spirits of the departed?

No, of course not. After a brief moment of awe, I realize the truth. I'm still in the land of the living and the living dead. The shadows are nothing more than the eddies in the water. And the light is coming from the sun shining on the Thames.

I howl mutely, water rushing down my throat, cursing Rage and this world that refuses to relinquish its hold on me. Then, with disgust, I kick for the surface.

I haven't drifted far from the London Eye. I can still see it gleaming above me, turning smoothly. No sign of Rage but I hurl a watery insult his way regardless. Then I swim towards the bank and pull myself ashore close to a bridge. I lie on the pebbly, rubbish-strewn bank, next to the remains of a bloated corpse, and make myself throw up. Then I get to my legs – understandably shaky – and stagger to a set of steps, then up to the South Bank.

I slump to the ground in front of what used to be the Royal Festival Hall. There are some restaurants and shops at this level, all closed for business now. There's also an open, ramped section where teenagers used to practice on their rollerblades and skateboards. To my surprise and bewilderment, judging by the rumble of small, hard wheels, people are still using it.

I look up, wondering where the teenagers have come from, and how they dare take to the outdoors like this, when the area must be riddled with zombies. Then I realize they have nothing to fear from the zombies because they're undead too.

There are at least five or six of them, maybe a few more. They have the blank expressions common to all revived, but some spark of instinct is urging them to act as they did when they were alive, and they trundle around the gloomy space on their skateboards, rolling down ramps, grinding along bars, slamming into the graffiti-covered walls.

The skateboarding zombies are nowhere near as graceful as they must have been in life. They fall often, clumsily, their hands and faces covered in scars, and they don't try any sophisticated jumps or moves. But it's still a strangely uplifting sight, and I start to clap stiffly, feeling somebody should applaud their efforts.

When they hear me clapping, the zombies instantly lose interest in their boards. The teenagers growl with hungry excitement and dart towards me, flexing their fingers, sniffing the air, thinking supper has come early.

They can't see the hole in my chest, and I'm too tired to push myself upright, so I wave a weary hand in the air and they spot the bones sticking out of my fingertips. With some disappointed grunting sounds, they return to their patch, pick up the skateboards and start listlessly rolling around again, killing time until it's night and they can set out in search of brains.

I watch the show for a few minutes, then make myself puke again and more water comes up. For once I'm glad I don't have functioning taste buds—the water of the Thames was never the most inviting, but it's worse than ever these days, stained with the juices and rotting remains of the bodies you often see bobbing along.

I'm still trembling with shock. My head is throbbing. I think

73

several of my ribs are broken. My left eyelid is almost fully shut now and won't respond to my commands. The fingers of both hands began to shake wildly when I stopped clapping and are spasming out of control.

I want to find Rage and rip his throat open, but in my sorry state I can't go anywhere at the moment. I just have to sit here, suffer pitifully and hope that I recover.

After a while, the clouds part. The sunlight stings my flesh and hurts my eyes, but helps dry me off. The warmth revives me slightly and the shakes begin to subside. When my hands are my own again, I roll onto my front, groaning, wishing the fall had put me out of my misery. I lie on the pavement like a dead fish, steam rising from my clothes, feeling sorry for myself, plotting my revenge on Rage.

A shadow falls across me. I look up through my right eye and spot a familiar face. Speak of the Devil…

"Have you checked out that lot?" Rage mutters, staring at the skateboarding teenagers.

"You're dead," I gurgle.

"Aren't we all?" he laughs, squatting beside me. "I half-hoped the fall would knock your brains out."

"Only half?" I wheeze.

"Yeah. Despite what you think, I don't enjoy killing. I do it when necessary and don't worry about it, but I never wanted to become a serial killer. I'm not out to break any records on that front."

"So why did you push me off?" I snarl, sitting up and shaking my head to get rid of the water in my ears.

"Making a point," he says. "I got sick of watching you mope around. Decided you needed a good, hard kick up the arse." Rage stands and starts rolling his arms again, still aching from the climb. "Dr. Oystein would have done all he could to save you up there. If I'd told him what I was planning, he would have thrown himself between us and stood up for you. He's not like me. He doesn't think you're worthless scum."

"That's your opinion of me?" I bristle.

Rage shrugs. "It's my opinion of us all. I never thought people were anything special. A grim, brutal, boring lot. You got the occasional interesting person, like those skateboarders over there—still cool, even in death. But most of us were only good for breeding, fighting and screwing up the planet."

"You're some piece of work," I snort.

"Just being honest," he smiles. "I'm a lot of bad things but I'm not a hypocrite. I always saw people for what they were, and I never thought that was very much. Dr. Oystein, on the other hand, sees the good stuff where I see the bad. He wants to make heroes out of me, you, Ivor and all the rest. I don't think he's gonna get very far with that, but I respect the mad old bugger for trying."

"I'm sure he'd be delighted to hear that," I sneer, getting up to face Rage.

"You need to accept the doc for what he is, or get the hell out of here," Rage says softly. "What I liked about you when we first met was that you stood up for your beliefs. You didn't like the way we were experimenting on the reviveds, so you refused to play ball. If you really don't trust Dr. Oystein, you need to do that again. I hate seeing you mope around. You're better than that. Stronger than that."

I stare at Rage, confused. He sounds like he's genuinely trying to help me. Or maybe he just wants me out of the way because I can see through him, because I know he's a threat.

"Listen up," Rage says. "These are your options: You can come back with me to County Hall, quit moaning and be a good little Angel like the rest of us. Or you can bugger off and look for a home elsewhere. Choose."

"Screw you!" I roar, finding my fiery temper again. "I don't have to do what you tell me!"

Rage grins. "Are you gonna tell me I'm not the boss of you?"

I laugh despite myself. "Bastard," I mutter, shaking my head.

"B," Rage says calmly, "I'm saying all this because I think of you as an equal. I wouldn't bother with most of the others. They're mindless sheep, like the zom heads were. You need to get with the program or get lost. If you're not happy here, go look for happiness somewhere else. You know the setup with Dr. Oystein. If you can't buy into it, get out now before you drive yourself mental."

77

"And go where?" I mumble. "Who'll look out for me apart from the doc and Mr. Burke?"

"That doesn't matter," Rage says. "You're not a child, so don't act like one."

"I'm more of a child than an adult," I argue.

"Nah," he says. "We've all had to grow up since we died. You can look after yourself. You survived on your own before you came to County Hall. You can survive on your own again."

"But I don't want to," I whisper.

"Tough. You're acting like a sulky little girl. Nobody else will tell you to your face. I don't know if they're being diplomatic or if they're afraid of losing you, given how few of us there are. But you're not doing anyone any good like this. Be honest with me—does part of you wish you'd cracked your head open when I pushed you off the Eye? Were you tempted to not crawl out of the river, to just let it wash you away and dump you somewhere nobody could ever find you?"

I nod slowly, hating him for knowing me so well, hating myself for it being true.

"It's a big world," Rage says. "I'm sure there's a place in it, even for a moody cow like you."

He turns to leave.

"Will you tell the others I said good-bye?" I call after him.

"No," he grunts without looking back.

I treat myself to a grim smirk. Then, accepting the decision that

Rage has helped me make, I push to my feet and cast one last longing glance in the direction of the London Eye and County Hall. Snorting water from my nose, I turn my back on them both and head off into the wilderness, abandoning the promise of friendship and redemption, becoming just another of the city's many lost, lonely, godforsaken souls.

ELEVEN

I limp along like a sodden rat, making my way past Waterloo before turning onto the Cut, once home to theaters, pubs and restaurants, now home only to the legions of the damned.

I don't look up much, just trudge along, head low, spirits even lower, cursing myself for being such a fool. Am I really going to turn my back on Dr. Oystein, the Angels, Mr. Burke and maybe the only sanctuary in the city that would ever accept someone like me? Can I really be that dumb?

Looks like it.

I make slow progress, hampered by my injuries and lack of direction. With nowhere to aim for, there's no need to rush. I'm itching like mad from the daylight but that doesn't deter me. I figure it's no more than a loser like me deserves. I don't even stop to pick up a pair of sunglasses or a hat.

I only pause when I reach Borough High Street. Borough Market is just up the road. That was one of London's most famous food markets. Mum dragged me round it once, to check it out. She decided it wasn't any better than our local markets, and a lot more expensive, so she never came back.

I'm sure the food stocks have long since rotted, and even if they haven't, food is of no interest to me these days. But most of Borough Market was a dark, dingy place, built beneath railway viaducts. I bet the area is packed with zombies.

Ever since I revitalized, I've looked for a home among the conscious. Maybe that's where I've gone wrong. I might fit in better with the spaced-out walking dead.

I turn left and shuffle along. As I guessed, the old market is thronged with zombies, resting up to avoid the irritating light of the day world. I nudge in among them, drawing sharp, hungry stares. I rip a hole in the front of my T-shirt to expose the gaping cavity where my heart used to be. When they realize I'm one of their own, they leave me be.

All of the shops are occupied but I find a vacant spot in a street stall. There are a few rips in its canvas roof, through which old rainwater drips, but it's dry and shaded enough for me. There are even some sacks nearby that I shake out and fashion into a rough bed.

When I'm as comfortable as I can get, I take off my clothes and toss them away. No point leaving them out to dry—I can easily pick up replacements later. It doesn't matter to me that I'm lying here naked. The zombies aren't watching and there's nobody else around. Hell, maybe I won't bother with clothes again. I don't really need them in my current state, except to protect me from the sun when I go out in the daytime. But if I stick to the night world as my new comrades do…

Dusk falls and the zombies stir. I head out with them to explore the city, interested to see where they go, how much ground they cover. I hunted with reviveds when I first left the shelter of the underground complex, but I never spent a huge amount of time in their company. I'd follow a pack until we found brains or, if they didn't seem to know what they were doing, I abandoned them and searched for another group.

Some of the zombies peel off on their own, but most stay in packs, usually no more than seven or eight per cluster. Hard to tell if they're grouped randomly or if these are old friends or family members, united in death as they were in life. They don't take much notice of one another – no hugging or fond looks – unless they communicate in ways that I'm not able to understand.

There's a woman in a wheelchair in one of the packs. Curious to see how she fares, I pick that one and stick with it for the whole night, trailing them round the streets of Borough and the surrounding area.

The zombie in the wheelchair has no problem keeping up with the others. Like the skateboarding teenagers, she remembers on some deep, subconscious level how she operated when alive.

They don't seem to be moving in any specific direction though, taking corners without pausing to think, circling back on themselves without realizing it, covering the same ground again. Their heads are constantly twitching as they stare into the shadows, sniff the air and listen for shuffling sounds that might signify life.

Rats are all over the place, foraging for food. They clearly don't consider the zombies much of a threat. And from what I see, they're right not to. One member of the pack catches a couple of rodents that were rooting around inside the carcass of a dog. He bites the head off each and chews them with relish. But those are the only successes of the night. The other zombies spend a lot of time stumbling after rats – the disabled woman launches herself from her wheelchair when she senses a kill, then sullenly drags herself back into it afterwards – but the fanged little beasts are too swift for them.

I know from chatting with the Angels that some zombies hole up in a particular place and stay there. Jakob did that when he was a revived, made his base in the crypt of St. Martin-in-the-Fields. But these guys don't have that inclination, and rather than head back to the market when dawn breaks, they nudge into a house just off the New Kent Road and make a nest for the day.

The disabled woman struggles to mount the step into the house. She moans softly but the others don't help her. Finally she throws herself forward, leaving the chair to rest outside until she reemerges when it's night again.

I stand by the wheelchair, scratching my head and scowling. I'd

hoped to make a connection with the zombies of Borough Market, slot in with them, find a place to call my own. As deranged as they are, many still function as they did in the past, driven by instinct and habit to behave as they did when they were alive. I thought the locals of the market might grow used to me, nod at me when they saw me, invite me to hunt and eat with them.

Doesn't look like that's the case, not if this pack is anything to go by. They hunt together for some unknown reason, but they have no real sense of kinship. It's every zombie for him or herself.

I could go back and try again, follow another group when night falls and see if they prove any brighter or more welcoming. But what's the point? I'm not the same as these poor, lost souls, and there's nothing to be gained by pretending that I am. Why the hell would they bother about an outsider like me when they don't even truly care about their own?

"You're a mug, B," I mutter. "And getting muggier every day."

With a sigh, I turn my back on the house of zombies and head off on my own again. If a home exists for me in this city, it isn't among the reviveds. Not unless I choose to go without brains for a week or two. I'd revert if I didn't eat, lose my mind, become one of them.

It doesn't sound like much of an option, but I consider it seriously as I hobble away. After all, what's worse, having company as a brain-dead savage, or remaining in control of your senses but feeling lonely as hell all the time?

TWELVE

I can't tolerate the daylight without clothes. My skin itches like mad and my eyes feel as if they're being burnt from the inside out. So I make for the shopping center in the Elephant and Castle. It's hardly a shopping mecca, but I find jeans, a T-shirt, a hoodie, a baseball cap and a jacket with a high collar. I pull on gloves and a few pairs of socks, finish up by tracking down some sunglasses.

I pick up a bottle of eye drops in a pharmacy, and squirt in some of the contents while there. My eyes would dry out without regular treatment. I wouldn't go blind, but my vision would worsen.

I'm also going to need heavy-duty files for my fast-growing teeth and bones, since I left all mine at County Hall, but I can sort those out later. It will be a few days before my teeth start to bother me. Hell, maybe I'll just let the buggers grow. I mean, if I don't have anyone to chat with, what difference does it make?

Loaded up with supplies, and having ripped a hole in the front of the hoodie and T-shirt to reveal my chest cavity, I head back up the New Kent Road. I'm still in a lot of pain from the fall off the Eye, but I can cope with it as long as I don't rush. I've dealt with worse in the not-too-distant past.

I come to a roundabout and swing left onto Tower Bridge Road. I take my time, checking out the windows of old shops, acting like a tourist. I pause sadly when I come to Manze's, an old-style pie-and-mash shop, where they soak the pies and mashed potatoes in a sickly green sauce, known as liquor. I wasn't into that sort of grub, but Dad loved it and he often talked about this place. He worked here for a while when he was a teenager. The stories he told were almost enough to turn me vegetarian. But as much as he'd spin wild tales about what went into the pies and liquor, he always swore this was the best pie-and-mash shop in London.

They used to do jellied eels too, and that reminds me of a guy I haven't thought about since finding my way to County Hall. Pursing my lips, I nod and carry on, a girl with a purpose, having made up my mind to go in pursuit of an actual target rather than just wander aimlessly.

As I'm coming to the junction of Tower Bridge Road and

Tooley Street, I draw to a surprised halt and do a double take. Then I remove my sunglasses, just to be absolutely sure.

There's a sheepdog in the middle of the road.

The dog is lying down, clear of all the buildings, keeping a careful watch on the area around it, though it must be hard with all that hair over its eyes. It has a beautiful white chest, running to gray farther back. Its hair is encrusted with dirt and old bloodstains. It pants softly and its tail swishes gently behind it.

I watch the dog for several minutes without moving. Finally, as if hypnotized, I start forward again, taking slow, cautious steps. The dog spots me and growls, getting to its feet immediately.

"It's all right," I murmur. "I'm not gonna hurt you. You're gorgeous. How have you survived this long? Are you lonely like me? I'm sure you are."

The dog scrapes the road with its claws and growls again, but doesn't bark. It must have figured out that barking attracts unwanted attention. Zombies don't like the daylight, but they'll come out if tempted. There aren't many large animals left in this city—most of them were long ago hunted down and torn apart by brain-hungry reviveds. This dog knows that it has to be silent if it wants to survive.

I stop a safe distance from the dog and smile at it. I want it to trust me and come to me. I picture the pair of us teaming up, keeping each other company, me looking out for the dog and protecting

it from zombies, while in return it helps me find fresh brains. This could be the start of a beautiful friendship.

"You and me aren't that different," I tell the dog. "Survivors in a place where we aren't wanted. Alone, wary, weary. You should have headed out to the countryside. You'd be safer there. The pickings might be richer here but the dangers are much greater. Why haven't you left?"

The dog stares at me with an indecipherable expression. I don't know if it sees me as a threat or a possible mistress. Hell, maybe it sees me as lunch! I doubt a dog like this could be much of a threat, but maybe it's tougher than it looks. It might have survived by preying on zombies, ripping their throats open, using the element of surprise to attack and bring them down.

I spread my arms and chuckle at the thought of being taken out by a sheepdog. "I'm all yours if you want me. I've no idea what zombies taste like, but anything must be better than rat."

The dog shakes its head. I know it's just coincidence, that it can't understand what I'm saying, but I laugh with delight anyway.

"Stay here," I tell it. "I'll fetch a bone for you to chew and a ball to play with."

I start to turn, to go and search the shops of Tower Bridge Road. As soon as I move, the dog takes off, tearing down the street to my right, headed east.

"Wait!" I yell after it. "Don't go. I won't hurt you. Come back. Please…"

But the dog isn't listening. I don't blame it. I wouldn't trust a zombie either, even one who can speak. It won't have lasted this long by taking chances. A creature in that position will have learnt to treat every possible threat as a very real challenge to its existence. Better to run and live than gamble and die.

I stay where I am for a while, reliving my encounter with the dog, smiling at the memory, hoping it will come back to sniff me out if I don't move. But in the end I have to accept that the dog has gone. I stare one last time at the spot where it was lying, then push on over the bridge, alone but not quite as lonely as I felt a few minutes before.

THIRTEEN

I glance at the HMS *Belfast* as I'm crossing the bridge, remembering the last time I wandered past. There were people on board then, heavily armed, and they opened fire as soon as they saw me. I'm too far away to see if they're still there, but I've no wish to go check. Hostile hotheads with guns are best left to their own devices.

As I draw close to the Tower of London, I recall the Beefeater who tackled me when I tried to sneak past. I wonder if he's still guarding the entrance, demanding a ticket from anyone who wants to enter. I bet he is. In an odd way I feel sorry for him. I'd like to take him some brains, a little surprise gift. I examine the corpses littered across the bridge, but their skulls have been scraped clean. Oh well, maybe another time.

I slowly make my way towards Whitechapel, then up Brick Lane. It feels like years since I was last here, even though it can't be more than...what? Two months or so, and I spent a good deal of that in the Groove Tube. I blame my skewed perception on not being able to sleep. Time moves much more sluggishly when you can't drop off at night.

I come to the Old Truman Brewery. The steel door is locked and there's no sign of life inside. But then there wouldn't be. Its artist-in-residence might be a God-obsessed nutter like Dr. Oystein, but he's smart enough to keep a low profile when at home. If he was in – which he probably isn't, since the sun's been up for quite a while and he's an early starter – I wouldn't know it from out here.

I don't knock on the door or bellow the artist's name. I could attract company if I did. Instead I lower myself to the ground, sit by the door and wait, patient as a spider. It might be a waste of time – a zombie might have snagged him ages ago – but I've nothing better to be doing.

The day passes slowly. I miss Master Zhang – time flew by when I was training with him – and the Angels. Even a sneering match with Rage was preferable to sitting on my own on a deserted street all day.

I don't see any other living or undead creatures, except for some rats who give me a wide berth. And insects of course. Lots and lots of insects. The streets are awash with them. Zombies have no interest in ant or cockroach brains, so they don't hunt them. They're

94

not creeped out by insects either – it takes a lot to startle a walking corpse – so they don't bother stamping on them or doing anything else to keep them in check.

I pass the hours counting the different types of insects that I see. I lose track a few times, until eventually I give up altogether. Then, late in the afternoon, I spot a man walking along, lugging an easel and whistling softly. I bet he doesn't know that he's whistling. He must be doing it subconsciously, unaware of the noise he's making. Even a soft whistle like that could bring a pack of zombies down on him, daylight or not.

He's almost at the door before he spots me. As soon as he does, he yelps, drops the easel and turns to flee.

"It's all right, Timothy," I call. "It's me, B."

He pauses and looks back uncertainly. "Mee-bee?"

"No, you dope." I stand, groaning as fresh pain flares in my battered bones. "It's me—B. Becky Smith. Remember?"

Timothy's expression clears. "Of course. B Smith, the talking zombie. I'm so delighted that you're still going strong. How are you? What have you been up to?"

Timothy bounds forward, smiling widely, hand outstretched. He's wearing the same sort of clothes as before, yellow trousers, a purple shirt, a tweed jacket. His brown hair is even longer than when I last saw him, shot through with streaks of paint. His eyes are still swamped by terribly dark circles in his long, thin face.

"You don't want to shake hands with me," I tut. "I'm not safe."

95

He comes to an immediate stop. "Oh, that's right. I was so excited to see you, I forgot. Silly me." He lowers his hand and chuckles. "As you can probably tell, I haven't spoken to anyone since we last met. I'm desperate for company. The painting keeps me going, but there's nothing like a good old bit of gossip to really stir the senses."

Timothy retrieves his easel and checks to make sure it hasn't been broken.

"I had hoped to see you sooner than this," he says, trying to phrase it lightly. "I thought you might come and visit me. When you didn't, I assumed you had either been welcomed with open arms by the soldiers you went off in pursuit of, or had been mown down by them."

"The latter," I grimace. "They opened fire when they realized I was undead, even shot a missile at me from a helicopter."

"But you survived and escaped?" Timothy claps enthusiastically. "Top-drawer! Where have you been since then? Why didn't you come back? I've painted some marvelous images. I'd love to share them with you."

"I've been busy," I mutter. "Things took a strange turn. Have you been over to County Hall since you started painting?"

"A few times," he nods. "I sketched it from the north bank of the river."

"You should wander south. You'd find a whole lot of interesting stuff to paint."

"That sounds intriguing," he purrs. "I look forward to hearing all about it. You are staying, aren't you? For a while at least?"

"If I'm welcome, yeah."

"Of course you're welcome," Timothy booms, bouncing to the door and getting out his key. "And you aren't the only one with news to share. I've played host to a most unique visitor since our paths last crossed. I'll have to introduce you, see what your opinion is, if you can make any more sense of it than I have."

I squint at him. "I thought you said you hadn't been talking to anyone since I left you."

"I haven't," he smirks. "This guest isn't much of a one for talking. But I think you'll be fascinated nevertheless. And who knows, maybe you'll manage to draw a response of some sort. I believe you might have more in common with the strange little dear than I have."

He laughs at my confused expression, then throws open the door and ushers me inside, politely asking me to wipe my feet on the way.

FOURTEEN

Timothy Jackson is an artist who survived the zombie attacks. Rather than lie low afterwards or flee the city as so many others did, he decided to make paintings of the downfall of London. Like Dr. Oystein, he thinks he has been handpicked by God, except in his case the Almighty only wants him to record images of the mayhem, not put a stop to it.

Once Timothy has stowed his equipment, he leads me upstairs, through a room of mostly blank canvases, to one crowded with finished works. It's even more jam-packed than it was the last time I was here. There's barely space to move.

"You've been busy," I note.

"Yes," he says with passion. "I feel like I've really hit my stride these last few weeks. I'm getting faster, without having to compromise my style. Here, look at this."

He shows me a large painting of a mound of bodies stacked in a heap, St. Paul's Cathedral rising behind them in the distance. Many of the faces are vague blobs and splashes of paint, but he's paid close attention to detail on a few of them, and also to the cathedral.

"Two days to complete," he says proudly. "That would have been at least a week's work just a couple of months ago, and I doubt I could have captured the expressions as clearly as I did. I'm improving all the time. Another year and who knows what I might be capable of?"

"How did the bodies end up in a pile like that?" I ask, staring at the morbid painting. "Did you gather them together?"

"Certainly not," Timothy huffs. "I paint only what I find. I never stage a scene. That would be cheating."

"Then how...?" I ask again.

"They were zombies," Timothy says softly. "They'd been shot, I assume by soldiers or hunters. If by soldiers, I imagine they stacked the bodies that way in order to come back and incinerate them at some point in the future. If by hunters, I suppose they did it so that they could pose for photos in front of their kills."

"Sometimes I think that your kind are worse than mine," I growl, recalling my own brush with the American hunter, Barnes, and his posse. "I've no problem with survivors killing zombies because of the threat we pose, but doing it for sport is sick."

"I agree," Timothy says. "Humans are far more dangerous than the

100

undead. I keep my head down when I hear gunfire. I know where I stand with zombies, but I never know what to expect from the living."

Timothy heads for the larder, washing his hands along the way, and prepares a simple meal for himself, cold beans on bread, some tinned carrots and a glass of red wine to wash it all down.

"Why don't you heat the food?" I ask.

"Zombies might pick up the smell," he explains. "I avoid cooking when I can. On those days when I simply *must* have a hot meal, I set up a barbecue in a park or public square and cook a big lunch. I tried cooking in a restaurant's kitchen once and was almost caught. I only barely got out alive."

Timothy has a mouthful of wine after he tosses away the tins, before tucking into his meager meal. He closes his eyes dreamily, savoring the taste, then cocks an eyebrow at me. "Are you sure you won't share a glass?"

"Apart from brains, I can't process anything," I tell him. "Liquids run clean through me. If I had any of that, I'd be sitting in a puddle by the end of the night."

Timothy clears his throat. "Ah. That might explain...I don't wish to be rude, but you might want to..." He wags a finger at me.

"What are you talking about?"

"When I was coming up the stairs behind you, I couldn't help but notice that the back of your trousers seemed rather damp."

My right eyelid flies wide open. (The left lid still doesn't work properly.) I feel behind and, sure enough, my fingers come away soaking.

"Damn it! I fell into the Thames yesterday and swallowed a load of water. I puked up most of it but obviously not all. Sorry about this."

"No need to apologize," Timothy says. "We all have our crosses to bear. Can I be of any assistance? There are plenty of towels and sheets here. If you wish, I could fashion you a..."

"...diaper?" I growl.

Timothy gulps and smiles sheepishly.

"Don't worry about it," I chuckle. "A wet bum is the least of my worries. I'll be happy with a towel to sit on, if that's all right with you."

"Absolutely." Timothy hurries off and comes back with two thick towels that he carefully places on a plastic chair. He waits for me to sit and give him the OK before taking his own seat and tucking into his food with a plastic knife and fork that he probably picked up from a takeout restaurant.

We chat as Timothy eats. He asks me where I went when I left him and I talk him through my trip to the West End, my run-in with Barnes and the other hunters, Sister Clare and her mad Order of the Shnax, their gruesome finale at the Liverpool Street Station, all the rest. I hesitate when I get to the Trafalgar Square part of the story, finding it hard to talk about even now.

"The soldiers drove you away?" Timothy asks sympathetically.

"No. They tried to kill me. They would have too – they had me pegged – except for Mr. Dowling and his mutants."

I expect Timothy to look blank, but to my surprise he knows

what I'm talking about. He was working on his last slice of bread, but now he lays it down and stares at me. "You've seen the mutants?"

"Yeah."

His voice drops. "And the clown?"

"Oh yeah. That's Mr. Dowling."

"You know his name?" Timothy sounds amazed.

"Of course. There's a big badge on his chest with his name on it."

"Really? I never got that close to him. And the man with the eyes? Do you know him too?"

I make a growling noise. "Him especially. He paid me a home visit back before all the madness started. I call him Owl Man. You've seen him too?"

Timothy nods, then stands and scurries away from the table, beckoning for me to follow. He leads me back to the room of finished canvases and roots through a pile stacked against one of the walls. I'd find it hard to distinguish between them since it's so dark – the windows are boarded over – but his eyes must have adjusted to the gloom over the months he's spent living and working here.

"I hung this up when I finished it," he mumbles as he searches, "but it gave me the shivers, so I took it down again. Those eyes followed me every time I passed, and not in a good way."

He produces a medium-size canvas and carries it to one of the rooms with no windows, the only places in the building where he dares turn on lights at night. He sets the painting down and stands back to study it, then slides aside to make space for me.

I don't recognize any of the buildings, just plain office blocks that could be anywhere in London. But there's no mistaking the horrific clown at the center of the painting, Mr. Dowling in all his dreadful finery. I'm familiar with the mutants surrounding him too, in their standard hoodies, with their rotting skin and yellow eyes.

And there's Owl Man, tall and thin, except for a ridiculously round potbelly. He has white hair and pale skin, but doesn't appear to be deformed in any other way. Except for his eyes, the largest I've ever seen, at least twice the size of mine. They're almost totally white, but with an incredibly dark, tiny pupil at the heart of each.

"If I hadn't seen him in the flesh, I wouldn't have believed his eyes could have been that big," I whisper.

"I know," Timothy says. "I almost made them smaller, to make them appear more in keeping with the size of his face, but I try not to distort reality when I paint."

"What were they doing?" I ask.

"Just talking. At least the man with the eyes was talking. The clown didn't seem to say much."

"He can't speak. He communicates with his mutants by making squeaking noises that they can interpret."

Timothy stares at me. "You seem to know a lot about them."

"Our paths have crossed a few times."

I study Mr. Dowling and Owl Man. The clown is the more frightening of the two, but Owl Man's eyes are unsettling—as Timothy said, they seem to follow me when I move. I wouldn't want to run into either of those eerie men on a dark night. Or a sunny day, come to that.

"Where did you see them?" I ask, turning away from the painting and trying to put it from my thoughts.

"Somewhere in the City," Timothy says. "I was wandering as normal, saw them in the distance and decided after one look that they weren't the sort of people I'd like to get better acquainted with. I managed to sneak close enough to sketch them. They didn't hang around for very long. As soon as they left, I hurried back here and worked up the painting. I didn't want to forget any of the finer details."

"When was this?"

He has to think. "Not long after you left. Maybe a week or so after."

"Have you seen them since?"

He shakes his head. "I haven't been looking either. There are some things that even I shy away from. I'm determined to capture this city in all its nightmarish glory, but I've a feeling I wouldn't last long if that clown and his crew were aware of me. I doubt they'd be as easy to shake off as the zombies if they gave chase."

"You've got that right," I sigh. "They let me go for some reason, but if they'd wanted to stop me, I don't think I could have done a hell of a lot about it."

"Do you know anything else about them?" Timothy asks. "Where they came from, what they are, what they might be planning?"

"No." I chuckle sickly. "But I know a man who does. At least he thinks he does. You're not the only guy working for God in London. And if this other prophet is to be believed, that clown is your direct opposite. If you were sent by God to paint the city as you find it, that nasty bugger was sent by the Devil to paint it black."

Timothy gapes at me, lost for words. I laugh at his expression and shake my head. "Come on, let's go back to the kitchen. I'll tell you all about it while you finish your food. Those creeps aren't worth missing a meal over."

FIFTEEN

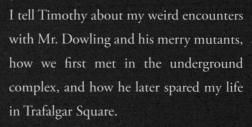

I tell Timothy about my weird encounters with Mr. Dowling and his merry mutants, how we first met in the underground complex, and how he later spared my life in Trafalgar Square.

"I don't know why he didn't kill me. Although, having said that, I haven't seen him harm any zombies. Maybe he only kills living people."

"That's a great comfort to me," Timothy sniffs.

"Don't worry," I grin. "You must have the luck of the Devil to have survived this long and, according to Dr. Oystein, Mr. Dowling is the Devil's spawn, so you're both in the same boat. He'd probably look upon you as a long-lost cousin."

"Why do you keep talking about the Devil?" Timothy frowns. "And who is this doctor you've referred to?"

"I'm coming to it," I tut. "What's the rush? We've got all night."

"You might have," Timothy says, "but I have to sleep, or had you forgotten?"

"Do you know," I say softly, "I had. It's been so long since I've slept that I've forgotten that it wasn't always this way, that there are people out there who don't have to sit up all night counting the circles on their fingers."

"Those are called whorls," Timothy informs me.

"Whorls my arse," I snort, then tell Timothy what happened after the battle between the soldiers and Mr. Dowling, finding the Angels in County Hall, training with them, Dr. Oystein's revelation about God's plans for him.

Timothy's last piece of bread remains uneaten, the beans soaking into it until it's a soggy mess. He's too engrossed in my story to focus on food. He hardly even sips his wine.

"Incredible," he murmurs when I finish. "What a load to take upon oneself. To bear responsibility for the future of the world... He has my admiration whether his story is true or not."

"Of course it's not true," I snap. "He's a nutter like Sister Clare and..."

I pause pointedly, waiting for Timothy to say wryly, "...and *me*?" But he only stares at me blankly. He's so sure of his calling that he finds it impossible to think that anyone might question him.

"Anyway," I chuckle, not wanting to burst poor Timothy's bubble, "I tried to overlook his God complex and fit in with the others, but in the end I couldn't stomach it, so I left."

Timothy nods slowly, then stares into his glass of wine, swirling the liquid around. He purses his lips, looks at the bread and beans, then picks up the plate and takes it to the sink to clean.

"Do you think Dr. Oystein is a liar or a madman?" Timothy asks while washing the plate in a bucket of cold water.

"Mad," I reply instantly. "He believes everything he says."

"You don't think he is trying to con you?"

"No."

Timothy stands the plate on a rack to dry, then turns and looks at me seriously.

"In that case, maybe he's right. Maybe he *is* a servant of God."

"Nah."

"How can you be so sure?" Timothy challenges me.

"Because..." I scowl. "Look, I don't want to piss you off, but it's rubbish, isn't it? God, the Devil, Heaven and Hell, reincarnation. I mean, I dunno, maybe there's some truth to some of it, but nobody can be sure. There have been so many different religions over the years, so many *truths*. How can one be right and all the others wrong?"

"I don't think it's about being absolutely right," Timothy says. "The main message of most religions is the same—be kind to other people, lead an honorable life, don't cause trouble. I've always seen

111

God as a massive diamond with thousands – maybe millions – of faces. We get a different view of the diamond, depending on which angle we look at it from. But there must be *something* there, otherwise what are we all looking at?"

"Maybe you're right," I huff. "I'm no expert, far from it. But there's more to why I left than the religious angle. It's the whole..." I grimace, not sure how to put my thoughts into words.

"Look," I try, "I've never seen ghosts, vampires or anything like that. This isn't a supernatural world. I believe in evolution. I'm sure there's life spread around the universe, more aliens out there than we can imagine. But I bet they're the same as us in that they just roll along wherever the universe pushes them, bound by the laws of nature as we are."

"My mother swore that she often saw the ghosts of her parents," Timothy murmurs. "They died when she was a girl, yet she never missed them because she saw so much of them as she grew up."

"Did she see fairies too?" I sneer.

"No," Timothy says calmly. "She was a mathematician. She had a doctorate from Cambridge. One of the sharpest minds in her field according to those who knew about such things. She wasn't especially religious. But she saw ghosts and accepted them as real. She even developed a mathematical equation to explain their relationship to the material world, though obviously I couldn't make head or tail of that."

"All right," I nod. "Sorry for poking fun at her. But that kind of proves my point. You say she came up with a formula to describe how ghosts work. I can accept that. There are all sorts of weird things in the world, but they can be explained with math and science. There's nothing miraculous about them."

"I disagree," Timothy says. "This *is* a world of miracles, of things that defy explanation, maybe even understanding. You're proof of that, a reanimated corpse, a girl whose soul has been restored. You might not believe in ghosts or vampires, but surely you believe in zombies?"

"Very clever," I growl as he smirks at me. "But there's nothing God-inspired about us. We're the result of an experiment gone wrong. I wasn't created by God, just as Dr. Oystein wasn't given heavenly orders to save the world from the Devil's henchman. This mess is our own fault, and if we're gonna fix it and put the world back together, we have to do it ourselves."

Timothy thinks about that. He finishes his wine and pours another glass. Takes a long, pleasing sip.

"What if you're wrong?" he asks quietly.

"I'm not."

"You can't be sure of that," he presses. "Using your own logic, no one can truly know the workings of the universe, or how much of a role God might play in our day-to-day lives. What if the creator *did* choose Dr. Oystein? There's no way of proving it, it's purely a matter of faith. But surely we all have to put our faith in someone. If you choose not to believe this particular prophet, fine, maybe you're right to doubt him. But why are you so set against even the possibility that he might be telling the truth?"

"Because it would stink if it was true!" I shout, then swiftly lower my voice, not wanting to alert any zombies that might be passing by outside.

"According to Dr. Oystein, God knew this was going to happen. He had decades of warning, and what did He do in all that time? Nothing, except give one guy the power to try and light the flames of a revival once the world had gone to hell. What sort of a God could do something like that to us?"

"A God who isn't the same as we are," Timothy says. "A God who has more to worry about than just our fate. A God who maybe has an eye on billions of worlds, who can't afford to spend His entire time trying to steer one particular species in the right direction. We can't understand the mind of God and, from what you say, Dr. Oystein doesn't claim to. He's simply doing what was asked of him. I can buy into that, a God who doesn't govern directly, but who tries to lend a helping hand. In a way I'd prefer that to a God who ruled by divine decree."

"The only person who lent Dr. Oystein a helping hand is himself," I jeer. "The voice in his head is his own. It has to be."

"It doesn't," Timothy insists. "This is a world of marvels and wonders. A world of miracles, if you wish to put it that way. In such a world, why can't God speak to Dr. Oystein or anyone else?"

"Because it's *not* a world of marvels," I snarl. "It's a world of science, math and nature."

"*And* miracles," Timothy says stubbornly. "There are things that science can't explain, wonders that confirm there is more to this universe than we know."

He downs the remains of his wine and sighs with contentment. Then he stands, a sparkle to his eyes.

"It's time I let you see my other visitor," he says. "Perhaps then you will be more inclined to accept the reality of the miraculous."

"If it's not Elvis Presley or Michael Jackson, I'll be very disappointed," I joke.

"It's neither of those fine men," he says. "But you'll be impressed regardless, I guarantee it."

Then he leads me from the room and up the stairs of the echoing old brewery in search of wonder.

SIXTEEN

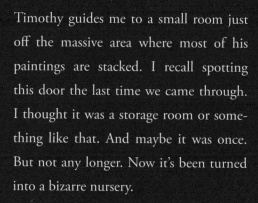

Timothy guides me to a small room just off the massive area where most of his paintings are stacked. I recall spotting this door the last time we came through. I thought it was a storage room or something like that. And maybe it was once. But not any longer. Now it's been turned into a bizarre nursery.

There's a crib in the middle of the room. Several mobiles hang from the ceiling. Lots of dolls and cuddly toys are stacked neatly in the corners. There's a large, inflatable dinosaur. Soft balls. A couple of activity gyms. A mix of blue and pink curtains draped around the walls.

"It's overkill, I know," Timothy says with a sheepish chuckle. "I just couldn't help myself. I had to have anything that

I thought my guest might enjoy. It's not like there are limits anymore. The shops are full of toys that will never be used. Why not spoil the poor creature? Although, having said that, I don't know if the little dear notices any of this."

"What are you talking about?" I start towards the crib, then stop dead. "Don't tell me it's a zombie baby. It is, isn't it? You've adopted a bloody undead baby!"

"B..." he starts to defend himself.

"What the hell were you thinking?" I shout. "I don't care how cute it might look—if it's a zombie, it's deadly. One scratch or nip and you're history. I can't believe you'd risk everything just so you can play daddy."

"It's not a zombie," Timothy says without losing his temper.

I stare at the crib suspiciously. "Are you telling me it's a real baby?"

"I wouldn't describe it that way either."

"You're not making sense," I scowl.

"That's why you have to go and look," he smiles.

I don't want to. Something about this feels wrong. I want to back out and get far away from here and whatever's in the crib. But fascination propels me.

I edge forward cautiously, ready to turn and run if I sense a threat. Then I come within sight of the baby and I freeze. My right eye widens and even my injured left eyelid lifts a bit. I feel the walls of reality crumbling around me, the world tilting on its axis, the fingers of a nightmare reaching out to grab me.

The baby is dressed in a long, white christening gown. Its tiny

118

hands are crossed on its chest. Its nails are sharper and more jagged than a normal baby's, but no bones jut out of the fingertips. Its feet are hidden by the folds of the gown.

Its face is a stiff mask, like a cross between a human's and a doll's, but there's nothing human about its mouth and eyes. The small mouth is open, full of tiny, sharp teeth. Its eyes are pure white balls, no pupils. Its eyelids don't flicker, though its lips twitch regularly and an occasional tremor runs through its cheeks.

A metal spike has been stuck through the baby's head. The spike enters the skull above the left eyebrow and the tip pokes out just behind the baby's left ear.

"Have you ever seen anything like that?" Timothy whispers.

"It's not real," I croak.

"I thought that too at first," he says. "I was sure it was a doll or a zombie. But it has a heartbeat. And if you watch closely, you'll see its chest rise and fall—it's breathing, just very slowly."

"It can't be real," I whisper. Then I add numbly, in answer to his question, "Yes. I've seen babies like that before."

"Where?" Timothy frowns.

"In my dreams."

I used to have a recurring nightmare when I was alive. I'd be on a plane and it would fill with babies that looked just like this one. In the dream they'd call me their mummy and clamber over me, ask me to join them, tear at me, bite, rip me apart, tell me I was one of them now.

That dream terrified me all of my life. I thought I'd finally escaped it when I stopped sleeping. But now it's somehow followed me out of the realm of the unreal and into the wide-awake world.

"You can't have dreamed of anything like this grisly beauty," Timothy says, dismissing my claim with a wave of his hand. "I took off its clothes when I brought it back. I wanted to see if it had been infected—I assumed it had to be a zombie, even with its heartbeat.

"It's not. No marks anywhere. No bites, scratches, nothing. Except for the spike through its head of course. I thought there might be undead germs on the metal, that the reason the child showed signs of life was because the zombie virus had first attacked its brain and then been inhibited by the position of the spike. And maybe there's something to that theory. But it doesn't explain…"

Timothy takes hold of the hem of the baby's gown and lifts it, exposing the child's feet, legs and more.

"Bloody hell!" I shout.

"…*this*," Timothy exhales softly.

The baby doesn't have any genitals. There's nothing but smooth flesh between its thighs.

"It doesn't have an anus either," Timothy says, and for some reason that makes me laugh hysterically. Timothy blinks with surprise and adds, "I can turn it over if you want to check."

I stop laughing abruptly. Then I moan, "Do me a favor and lower the gown. I've seen enough."

Timothy lays the gown back in place and smooths down the hem.

121

"What is it?" I hiss.

"I don't know," Timothy says. He waits a few beats, then grins wickedly. "It's a *miracle*."

"No," I choke. "There's nothing miraculous about a freak like that. Diabolical, maybe."

"Don't say such things," Timothy frowns. "It's only a baby. It can't help the way it's been put together."

"But who created it?" I ask, voice rising again. "Where did it come from? How can it live with a spike through its head?"

"I don't know," Timothy says, smiling lovingly at the white-eyed baby. "But that's not the only remarkable thing. I found the child maybe three weeks ago. It was lying in the road close to the Aldgate East Tube entrance, near Whitechapel Art Gallery. That was one of my favorite galleries. Did you ever visit it?"

I shake my head, unable to glance away from the unnatural child.

"The baby hasn't eaten in all that time," Timothy continues. "I tried to feed it milk and biscuits when I first rescued it, but it wouldn't swallow. I was going to poke a tube down its mouth and force-feed it, but I decided there was no point keeping the poor creature alive in such a pitiable condition. So I sat back and left it to nature, waiting for it to die.

"As you can see, it hasn't. It's in the same condition today as it was when I found it."

"But how?" I ask again. "What is it? Where did it come from?"

"Like you, I've been asking those questions over and over,"

Timothy says. "No answers have presented themselves. For the first few days I didn't leave its side. I stood watch, waiting for it to die, putting my work on hold. When I saw that it wasn't going to pass away, I returned to my normal routine, though I spend most of my nights in here now. I've started reading stories to it. I don't know if it can hear me or understand what I'm saying, but I like reading out loud."

Timothy looks around at everything that he's gathered and sighs. "Like I said, I know it's overkill, but I can't stop bringing back presents. I guess I was lonelier than I realized."

"Has it ever said anything?" I ask, moving closer to the baby, staring at its teeth – *fangs* – and pale white lips.

"No. Its mouth moves but always silently. What age do you think it is? When do babies start to speak?"

I can't answer those questions. I don't really care.

"The babies in my dreams could speak," I whisper. "I need to know if this one can, if it says the same sort of things that they used to."

"How could it?" Timothy scoffs. "This isn't from your dreams. It's real."

"Still..." I reach towards the baby.

"What are you doing?" Timothy snaps.

"I'm going to pull out the spike."

"The hell you are!" he shouts, pushing me away.

"Easy," I say, putting my hands behind my back, wary of accidentally scratching and infecting him. "I don't want to hurt it. But I have to find out."

"You're not going anywhere near that spike," Timothy growls. "It holds the poor thing's brain in place. If you pull out the spike, you'll kill it."

"I wouldn't be so sure of that," I mutter. "But even if I do, so what? Look at it, Timothy. That's no normal baby. Whatever it is, wherever it came from, it's not one of us. One of *you*," I correct myself.

"Even so, it's alive and defenseless and I've sworn to protect it," Timothy says grandly.

"The damn thing has a spike through its head," I remind him. "It's a bit too late for protection."

"Spike or no spike, it's still alive," Timothy argues.

"But what sort of a future does it have?" I press. "For all we know it's in agony and is silently begging for someone to end its pain. Maybe it will recover if we remove the spike. Who knows how a thing like this might function? For all we know, it doesn't even have a brain.

"It has no quality of life," I say, taking a step towards the crib. Timothy doesn't try to stop me this time. "If we leave it as it is, it will definitely die in the end, whether it needs food or not. This way it has a chance. We might save it."

"Do you really believe that?" Timothy whispers.

"Yeah," I lie.

"I only want what's best for the little darling," he sighs.

"This is the way forward," I assure him. "We can cover the hole with a bandage if we need to, maybe even stick the spike back in. It's risky, I won't deny it, but what choice do we have?"

124

"We could stand by and not interfere," Timothy says, then shakes his head. "No. You're right. That would be selfish of me. This way it has a chance. Go on, B. I'll support you. I won't blame you if it goes wrong."

I stretch out a trembling hand and grip the spike above the baby's eye. I stare again at that pure white orb, remembering the babies in my dreams, how their eyes turned red when they attacked me. I gulp. Tighten my grip. And pull.

The spike comes out with very little resistance. There's a small sucking sound as it clears the clammy flesh. Blood oozes out of the hole, but slowly, not in huge amounts. A few bits of brain trickle from the spike.

Timothy and I stare at the baby. Neither of us says a word.

Nothing happens.

Then, maybe a full minute after I've withdrawn the spike from the baby's head, it shudders. Its arms uncross and its fingers claw at the blankets beneath it. As I watch with disbelief and horror, its eyes turn red, as if filling with blood, and it starts to scream in a terrifyingly familiar, tinny voice. "*mummy. mummy. mummy. mummeeeeeEEEEEEE.*"

SEVENTEEN

The baby keeps squealing, the same word repeated without even a pause for breath, calling for its *mummy*. The high-pitched noise cuts through me, making me wince and grind my teeth. Timothy is staring slack-jawed at the whining, red-eyed child.

"Make it stop," I bark, covering my ears with my hands.

"How?" Timothy asks.

"Stick the spike back in its head."

"No," he says, face turning a shade paler at the thought. "We can't do that. Let's find it a pacifier."

He lurches to a shelf stacked with baby stuff. He roots through the neat pile until he finds one. He hurries back and leans over the crib, cooing to the hellish baby, "There, there. It's all right. We'll take care of you. No need to cry. Does it hurt? We'll make the pain go away. You're our little baby, aren't you?"

"Less of that crap," I snort, shuddering at the thought of being mother to such an unearthly creature. "Just shut the damn thing up."

"Be nice, B," Timothy tuts, then yelps and takes a quick step away from the crib. "It tried to bite me!"

"Oh, give it to me," I snap, nudging him aside and taking the pacifier from him. I bend over, fingers of my left hand extended to widen the baby's mouth if necessary. Before I can touch its lips, the tiny creature's head shoots forward and its fangs snap shut on the bones sticking out of my middle and index fingers.

"Let go!" I roar with fright, and try to pull my hand free. The baby rises with my arm, dangling from the bones, fangs locked into them, chewing furiously, head jerking left and right.

I wheel away from the crib, shaking my arm, trying to dislodge the monstrous infant. Timothy is yelling at me to be careful, not to drop the child. I swear loudly and try to hurl the baby loose.

I lose my balance, crash into the inflatable dinosaur and stumble to my knees. As I push myself to my feet again, the baby chews through the bones, drops to the floor and collapses on its back. It immediately resumes screaming for its mummy.

"Bloody hell!" I pant, retreating swiftly. My hand is trembling.

"I told you it wasn't a good idea," Timothy says smugly. "It obviously doesn't want a pacifier, and with teeth like that, who are we to argue?"

"Sod what it wants," I snarl. "We have to shut it up."

"You can try again if you wish," Timothy chuckles. "Personally I like my fingers the way they are. Those teeth are amazing. I wonder what they're made of?"

"You go on wondering," I growl, crossing the room to pick up the spike. "I'm putting a stop to this."

"No," Timothy says sternly. "You can't do that."

"I bloody well can," I huff, advancing on the wailing baby.

Timothy steps in my way and crosses his arms.

"Move it, painter boy. I'm not playing games."

"Neither am I," he says. "You're not sticking that into the baby's head. You might kill it."

"Do I look like I care?"

"No. That's why I can't let you proceed. You're not thinking clearly. You're upset and alarmed, understandably so. But when you calm down, you'll see that I'm right. This is a living baby, calling for its mother. It's afraid and lonely, probably in pain and shock. We have to comfort it, not treat it like a rabid animal that needs to be exterminated."

"Didn't you see what it did with those teeth?" I roar, waving my gnawed fingerbones at him.

"Yes, but to be fair, you were attacking it. I would have bitten in self-defense too if you'd come at me like that."

"But you wouldn't have been able to chew through my bones," I note angrily.

"So its teeth are tougher than ours," he shrugs. "What of it? That's no reason to risk the poor thing's life. I can't let you stick that spike in again."

"How are you going to stop me?" I challenge him.

"Just by standing here," he says. "You'll have to wrestle me out of the way to get to the baby. If you do that, you'll almost certainly scratch me. That would mean my death. I don't think you'd kill me so recklessly."

"I'm a zombie," I say softly, moving closer, going up on my toes to give him the evil eye. "You don't know how my mind works, what I'd do if pushed."

"Perhaps," he says. "But I'm willing to take that chance. This baby needs our help and love. It's our duty to study it, protect it, nurse it back to health. It can talk, so perhaps it can answer our questions when it recovers, tell us where it came from, what it is."

"The babies never wanted to discuss much in my dreams," I sniff. "They only wanted to slaughter me."

"But this isn't a dream," Timothy says. "The baby simply reacted the way any cornered creature would. Look at it lying there now, helpless as a . . . well, as a *baby*. It doesn't pose a threat to us."

I shake my head stubbornly. "It's a monster. Of course it poses a threat."

"You're a monster too," Timothy smiles. "But I'm not afraid of you and I'm not afraid of the baby either. We can be its foster parents."

I stare at him oddly. "What, become a couple?"

"Of course not," he smiles. "But we could be partners and raise it together."

"Why would I want to do that?"

"Salvation," he says softly, stepping aside when he sees me hesitate. "My paintings have kept me busy, and I plan to carry on doing them for as long as I can. But I lost a lot that defined me as a human when the world fell. Maybe this baby is a way for me to retrieve some of my humanity, and for you too.

"I haven't been truly happy since the zombies took control. Content, yes, with my artistic output, but happy? No. I don't think you're happy either. This is a chance for us to put the darkness behind us for a while."

"What if you're wrong?" I croak. "What if the baby's as monstrous as it looks and only drags us further into trouble?"

Timothy shrugs. "Isn't it worth taking that risk?"

I have a clear line of attack now. If I darted at the baby, Timothy wouldn't be able to stop me. I could smash its skull with the spike, crush its throat, rip it to pieces.

But how could I live with myself if I did that to a baby? I've sunk lower than I ever dreamed I could, murdered, scraped heads bare of their brains, lived among the fetid and the damned. But to butcher a baby just because I'm afraid of it, because I had nightmares about things like it when I was younger...

"That freak will be the ruin of us both," I pout.

"Perhaps," Timothy grins, understanding from my expression that I can't follow through on my threat. "But we have to take that chance. Now let's see what we can do to help this poor lamb. Maybe it will stop screaming if we put it back in its crib, tend to its wound and show that we mean no harm. I'm sure that with a little TLC it will respond to our ministrations and –"

Timothy stops. He had started to bend to pick up the baby, but now he turns and stares at the doorway, into the gloom of the large room beyond. He cocks his head and frowns.

"Do you hear that?" he whispers.

"What?"

I step up beside him, trying to focus. The screams of the baby – "*mummy. mummy. mummy.*" – fill my head and I find it hard to tune them out.

Timothy moves through the doorway as if sleepwalking, eyes wide, a slight tic in his left cheek. I follow and close the door behind me, muffling the sounds of the baby.

I zone in on the new noises. They're coming from outside the building. Loud, scratching sounds, similar to a nail being dragged across a blackboard, only much sharper, and not one nail but dozens at the same time.

"What is it?" I ask softly, although part of me has already guessed. I'm not stupid. As I've stated proudly on more than one occasion in the past, I can put two and two together.

"Zombies," Timothy says, and his expression never alters.

"They've heard the baby. They're climbing the walls." He points to the boarded-over windows with a surprisingly steady finger. Unlike the thick boards nailed over the windows on the ground floor, those up here were designed primarily to keep in the light, not keep out the ranks of the living dead. With all the oversized windows in this place, that would be impossible. This is a gallery, not a fortress. Anonymity was its only real defense.

"They know that we're here," Timothy says. "They're going to break in."

And with those few calm words he pronounces his death sentence.

EIGHTEEN

"We have to get out of here!" I roar. "Where are the exits?"

Timothy shakes his head wordlessly. He's staring at the boards covering the windows. He looks more thoughtful than scared.

"Timothy!" I scream, wanting to grab and shake him, but afraid of piercing his skin with my bones.

"The roof," he murmurs.

"No good," I grunt. "They're climbing the walls. They can get to us in seconds on the roof. We have to go down to the ground floor, escape out the back, try to lose them on the streets."

The first zombies start pounding on the glass and it shatters. They tear into the boards, ripping them loose. I catch glimpses of bones, fingers, faces, fangs.

Windows run the whole length of this room. The boards on pretty much all of them begin to crack and snap beneath the strain. There must be dozens of zombies out there, maybe more.

"Come on," I shout, heading for the stairs.

"The baby," Timothy says.

"You've got to be bloody joking!"

"The baby," he says, stubbornly this time. "I won't leave it to them."

"You can't save it," I growl. "Its cries are what's drawing them. If we take it with us, they'll follow the noise."

"But it's a baby..." he says miserably.

"No baby of our world," I snort, then run with a wild idea. "Maybe one of the zombies is its mother. That might explain why it looks so strange. She might have been pregnant when she was turned. Maybe it was born after she died."

"That sounds feasible," Timothy nods.

"If that's the case, they might accept it as their own. It might find a home with them."

"Or they might rip it to shreds," Timothy notes glumly. "Maybe zombies stuck the spike through its head in the first place."

I roll my eyes. "Either way, the baby's going to be theirs in a minute. We can't stop them. We can put up a pointless fight and get torn apart or focus on our own necks and maybe make it out of here. Your choice, Timothy. I already died once. If they kill me again, it's not that big a deal."

I wait for him to make up his mind. I'll stick by him no matter

136

what he decides. He's my friend and I want to do whatever I can to protect him, even though I know I can't.

Timothy licks his lips, torn between wanting to be a hero and knowing his limits. There's a loud snapping noise and the first of the zombies tumbles through the broken boards.

"God forgive us!" Timothy cries and races for the stairs, leaving the screeching baby to whatever fate has in store for it.

We pound down the stairs, taking them two or three at a time. I'm in agony, my broken ribs digging into my flesh and organs with every lurching movement. I ignore the pain as best I can, trying to focus on Timothy and getting him out of here before the zombies catch up.

We race through the room of blank canvases and supplies, the sound of the snapping boards above following us like the beat of tom-toms.

"Almost there," Timothy pants, overtaking me as I stumble. "There's a door at the rear of the building which I earmarked for an eventuality such as this. It opens quickly and quietly. If we can get outside, there's a good chance we can –"

He stops.

"Keep going," I snap. "This is no time to –"

I stop too.

We've come to a short set of steps. They lead to the main downstairs room, a huge, open space. The windows at this level were boarded over professionally to keep out zombies. This should be the safest room in the entire building.

It's not.

The boards have held. So has the front door. But there are other doors. I'm sure that Timothy and the people who occupied this building before he came here did all that they could to secure those entrances. But there must have been a weak link somewhere, a chain that snapped, a lock that broke, hinges that crumbled.

Because the room is thick with zombies.

They stand silently, an army of them, motionless, faces raised to the ceiling, as if trying to determine exactly where the shriek of the baby is coming from.

Timothy trembles, losing his cool at last.

"Easy," I whisper. "They're not moving. They look like they're in some kind of a trance. We might be able to slip through them."

I take a step down.

No response.

Another step.

Not a single zombie moves.

A couple more, then I stretch out my right foot to take the final step.

As soon as my toes touch the ground, the neck of every zombie snaps down as they lower their heads in perfect timing. They bare their teeth and snarl, then surge towards us without breaking ranks.

"Bugger!" I scream, turning to start back up the stairs. "Come on!" I roar at Timothy. "We've got to try for the roof."

"We'll never make it," he sobs, but tears along after me.

We hurry through the room of supplies. Timothy is praying

aloud, his words coming fast and furious, sounding like gibberish. We reach the stairs to the main gallery. They're clear. No sign of any zombies. I silently thank God and ask Him for another minute, sixty seconds, that's all we need. If we can make it to the roof, Timothy can cling to my back and I can either leap to another roof or all the way to the ground. My legs should be able to take a drop like that. I might break a few bones but it won't scramble my brain. Even if I can't carry on, Timothy can escape by himself. The zombies won't harm me once he's gone. He can return for me later. A minute. That's all we need. That's not too much to ask for, is it?

Apparently it is.

We're not even halfway up the stairs when the zombies from the upper floor come spilling towards us. They've made it through the windows and boards. They stagger down the steps, arms outstretched, leering hungrily.

Timothy screams and turns to flee, but more zombies are coming up the steps, having tracked us from the room below.

We're screwed.

I reach out to grab Timothy and pull him in tight, meaning to bite his neck, figuring the best I can do for him now is to end it quickly and maybe give him a chance of revitalizing. I was injected with Dr. Oystein's vaccine when I was a child. That's why I recovered my wits when I was turned into a zombie. Maybe I can pass some of my revitalizing genes on to Timothy. I doubt he stands much of a chance but it's better than none at all.

But I'm too late. A zombie tackles me before I can strike and I fall to the steps, driven down by the weight of my assailant. Others throw themselves on top of me, burying me at the bottom of a pile of bodies.

"Timothy!" I shriek.

"Good-bye, B," he says sadly as the first of the zombies pins him to the wall and scrapes at his stomach. Others swarm around him, digging into the flesh of his arms and legs with their bony fingers. Timothy screams, a cry of pure agony and loss. He screams again as zombies rip chunks of flesh from his body with their teeth. They're not concerned about converting him—they want to finish him off.

Madness fills Timothy's eyes, but with a supreme effort he shrugs it off for one last instant and locks gazes with me as I stare at him helplessly from my position on the floor.

"Take care of my paintings," he wheezes pleadingly.

Then a zombie digs its fingers through Timothy's eyes. He has time to scream once more before the zombie breaks through to his brain and starts scraping it out and cramming pieces into its foul, eager mouth.

There's no more screaming after that. Timothy Jackson is dead and gone. And all I can do is wait for the zombies to rip me apart and maybe send my soul to join Timothy's in the peaceful, welcome realms beyond.

NINETEEN

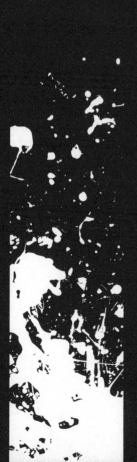

The zombies piled on top of me poke and maul me, unable to strike cleanly because so many are pressed in around me. Then, as the others retreat from Timothy's bloody, shredded remains, those holding me down fall still. I hear them sniffing and I sense them cocking their heads, listening for a heartbeat. When they realize I'm dead, they go slack and start pushing themselves off me, no longer viewing me as either a threat or a tasty treat.

I rise with a groan, prop myself against the wall and stare miserably at all that is left of my artistic, eccentric friend. He was a crazy but sweet guy. He deserved better than this. But then so did billions of others. In this world of savagery and death, there's only what you get. *Deserve* doesn't come into it anymore.

The zombies don't budge. Those with nothing to eat aren't moving at all, just standing on the steps, faces raised again, looking towards the top of the stairs. They're all silent, motionless, eyes fixed on the same spot. It's eerie.

I think about trying to slip away, but they reacted aggressively the last time I did that. I figure it's safer to give it some time, see what happens.

I don't have to wait long. After about a minute, the zombies part, moving to both sides of the stairs, forming a bizarre guard of honor. They don't lower their heads as they shuffle over, gazes fixed on that same spot at the top of the stairs.

This is really freaking me out. I ready myself to run, sod the consequences. I'd rather be torn apart than remain among this lot. There's something sinister going down and I don't want to be here when it hits.

But I'm too late. Even as I'm stretching out my foot to take my first tentative step, a pack of zombies appears at the top of the stairs. They march three abreast. They're holding their arms above their heads, linked together. Those at the front are children, then women, then men, arranged according to height, the way they would be if marching in a parade.

The children pass me, two rows of them. Then the women, three rows. Then the men start to come past. The first half-dozen have their arms linked over their heads, the same as the women and children. So have the men in the last two rows. But those between are holding something up high, as if it was a holy relic. Except this is no religious artifact.

It's the crib from the baby's room.

As they draw level with me, the procession comes to a stop. I'm staring at the side of the crib. As I watch, the baby crawls to the bars, then pulls itself up until it's standing. It looks calmer than it did before, a slight smile in place. It's stopped screaming. Its unblinking eyes are white again, the red sheen having receded.

The baby is looking at me.

"What the hell are you?" I moan.

"*mummy*," the baby says softly.

"No," I wheeze, shaking my head, denying the claim. "I'm not your mother. I'm nothing to you."

The baby's expression doesn't alter, but its hands move and it pulls the bars farther apart, as if they were made of rubber. When the space is wide enough, the baby gently pokes its head through the gap. Its smile spreads.

"*join us mummy*," it says in its tinny, unnatural voice.

"No," I say again. My throat has tightened. If I could cry, I'd be weeping now.

The baby frowns. "*don't be frightened mummy. you're one of us. come with us mummy.*"

"I'm not one of you!" I scream. "I don't even know what the hell you are."

The baby giggles. "*yummy mummy. come.*"

"I'm not coming anywhere," I snarl. "You're a bloody freak. I wouldn't spit on you if you were on fire."

The baby seems to consider that. After a long pause, it draws its head inside the crib and bends the bars back into place. It looks disappointed.

The zombies start to move again, down the stairs. The baby turns its face away and I think it's over. Then they stop. The baby's neck swivels and its nightmarish features swim back into view. Remembering the dreams I used to have, I expect it to tell me that I have to die now. I brace myself, waiting for the baby to climb the bars and hurl itself at me from the top of the crib.

But this baby doesn't appear to have murder on its mind. Its eyes don't redden and its mouth doesn't split into a vicious sneer. In fact it looks sad, maybe even lonely. And when it addresses me again, it's not to threaten or scare me. Instead it whispers something that makes me gape at it with bewilderment.

"*we love you mummy.*"

With that, the macabre infant faces forward. It looks like a tiny prince or princess on a very grand throne, borne along by a team of devoted courtiers. It giggles, then the zombies resume their march. At the bottom of the stairs they process through the room of supplies, then down the small set of stairs to the ground-floor room and the exit.

The zombies around me hold their position until the retinue

passes from sight. Then they fall in behind and follow the crib and its carriers out of the building. A minute later, every single one of them has gone, and all that's left behind are the paintings, Timothy's scattered remains and the most incredulous, slack-jawed girl the world has ever seen.

TWENTY

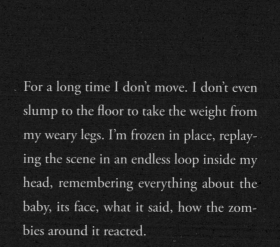

For a long time I don't move. I don't even slump to the floor to take the weight from my weary legs. I'm frozen in place, replaying the scene in an endless loop inside my head, remembering everything about the baby, its face, what it said, how the zombies around it reacted.

It was controlling them. It called for them when I removed the spike. They came in their hundreds, rescued it, took it wherever it told them to take it. Like the mutants who work for Mr. Dowling, the baby somehow has the power to make zombies do what it wants.

But it didn't have the power to bend *me* to its will. I was able to resist its call to follow it back to its lair.

Or was I? Maybe it simply let me go.

It called me its mummy. It said it loved me. Maybe it thinks I really am its mother. It might have the potential to control me, but chose not to exercise it because of the bond it believes we share.

This is insane.

This is impossible.

This is terrifying.

Eventually I force myself to move. I struggle back up the stairs, taking them one slow step at a time. I shuffle into the nursery and gaze at the toys, the mobiles, the space where the crib stood. I spot the spike on the floor and seriously think about picking it up and driving it through my own skull. Escape from this world of horrors tempts me more than ever before. How can I witness something like this and carry on as if all is well or can ever be made well again?

Ultimately I reject suicide, fearful that it might not achieve anything. The baby and its clones originally tormented me in my dreams. Now they've chased me into this world. Who's to say they couldn't follow me into the afterlife too?

I limp back down the stairs to the room of supplies and search for a bag. I find a suitable one without too much difficulty, empty it of its contents, then retrace my steps and gather up the remains of poor Timothy. I hate having to do this – it would be much simpler to just leave – but I feel like I owe him. I brought the zombies down upon him. If I hadn't come here, he might never have tried to pull the spike from the baby's head. He could have gone on living and painting for months, maybe years, until his luck ran out. He's dead because of me. The least I can do is tend to his remains and give him some sort of a halfway decent burial.

I pick up every last scrap of Timothy, clothes as well as bones, skin and organs. I bag them all. After a while, I realize I'm making a low moaning noise, the closest I can get to crying. I don't make myself stop.

Job complete, I start to drag the bag down the stairs. I pause when I spot the trail of blood that I'm leaving behind. The bag isn't blood-proof. The bits inside are leaking.

I find another couple of bags, more resistant to liquids than the first, and triple-bag the corpse. That does the trick. There are no stains now.

I lug the grisly package to the front door, then climb the stairs once more, get a bucket of water and a mop and go to work on washing away the blood. Timothy's last request was that I looked after his paintings. The blood would attract flies and insects, maybe larger creatures like rats, which might attack the canvases. If I survive long enough, I plan to come back here every month or so, dust and clean, take care of the paintings, do all that I can to maintain the legacy of Timothy Jackson. That probably won't prove much of a comfort to him where he's gone, but it's all I can do to honor his memory.

When I'm finished cleaning, I return to the bag by the door and sit beside it. I don't want to go out until night has passed and day has dawned. Too many zombies at large in the darkness. Too many shadows in which the living dead and killer babies can hide.

I spend the night silently thinking, reexamining the world, my life, the very nature of the universe.

I thought I had it figured out. I told Burke, Rage and Timothy that this wasn't a world of miracles. If God existed, He didn't get involved in what was happening to us. I couldn't see His hand at work anywhere. We were on our own, I was sure of it.

The baby suggests to me that I was wrong. For years I dreamed of babies just like this one. They looked the same, wore the same clothes, had the same eyes and fangs, even said the same things.

"*join us mummy.*"

"*don't be frightened mummy.*"

"*you're one of us.*"

How could I have dreamed about them, never having seen such a demonic baby until tonight? How could my nightmares have been so accurate, correct down to the tiniest detail? Did God send me visions of the future, to prepare me for what was to come, so that I would realize He was real and put my faith in others that He had chosen? Does He want me for His team?

I don't know. I want to believe – it would be so wonderful to think that I understood everything, and had been handpicked by such a powerful being – but I can't, not a hundred percent. What I can do, however, after my run-in with the baby, is doubt. Not Dr. Oystein but myself. There are enough questions in my mind now to make me far less sure that the doctor is deluded. I'm not saying I'm taking him at his word about God speaking to him. But I'm willing to listen to him now, to give him a chance, to put my faith in him.

Hell, from where I'm standing after my experiences tonight, it makes as much sense as anything else in this wickedly warped world.

TWENTY-ONE

The sun rises and I haul Timothy's remains outside. I shut the door behind me and hide the keys in the yard of the old brewery. I only remember the other door – the one the zombies used to get into the building – on my way down Brick Lane. I wince and think about retrieving the keys, going back inside and searching for the other entrance, to seal it.

"Sod it," I mutter. "Life's too short."

I'll do my best for Timothy's paintings, but I'm not going to go overboard. Right now I'm exhausted. I'm not in my worst-ever physical state – that was after Trafalgar Square – but mentally I'm beat. I reckon I need to spend at least a month in a Groove Tube to recover. I can't face even the minor challenge of searching for an open door.

I'll do it the next time I come. If zombies or other intruders beat me to the punch, sneak in before I return and wreak havoc, tough.

I know where I want to take Timothy. I can't be sure but I think he'd like it. Too bad if he doesn't because he can't complain now.

I lug the bag through the streets, shivering and straining, itching beneath the sun—I have my hoodie pulled up but I forgot the hat and jacket. It should be a short walk – no more than five or ten minutes any normal time – but it takes me half an hour. I don't mind. I'm not in a rush.

Finally I reach my destination. Christ Church Spitalfields, one of London's most famous churches, always popping up in films and TV shows about Jack the Ripper. It's a creepy place, but beautiful in a stark way, and I think Timothy would have appreciated it. He loved the East End. I don't recall him mentioning Christ Church, but I'm confident he would have raved about it if the subject had come up.

There's a small, grassy area in front of the church, some headstones dotted about. I find a nice spot for Timothy, somewhere that looks like it gets a lot of sun, then go in search of a shovel. I find one in a shop in Spitalfields Market, a colorful designer spade for ladies who wanted to look chic in their garden. There are no zombies in any of the shops or restaurants. I suppose they abandoned their resting places in response to the baby's call.

It takes me longer than I thought to dig the hole, and not just because I'm so drained. Digging a grave is hard work. I wouldn't have liked to do this for a living in the old days.

I go down a couple of meters, not wanting to take chances and come back this way to find the grave dug up and raided by wild animals or zombies. When I'm happy with the depth, I haul myself out and lie on the grass for a while, an arm thrown across my face to shield my eyes from the sunlight.

Rising, I consider removing Timothy's remains from the bags, but why bother? Let them serve as his coffin. Probably not the way he would have liked to be buried, but better than nothing.

I lower the bags into the grave, then stand over it hesitantly, trying to think of the proper prayers to say.

"Ashes to ashes, dust to dust," I murmur, but I can't remember the rest, and that doesn't seem like enough. In the end I recite a few Hail Marys and an Our Father.

"I hope you can carry on painting in the next world," I conclude weakly, then fill in the grave, silently bid Timothy one last farewell and glance at the spire of Christ Church. Shivering, I wonder if there really is a God or if I'm just grasping at straws, if the babies of my nightmares actually were a sign or just some freakily incredible coincidence. Am I right to trust Dr. Oystein, or am I making the worst mistake of my life?

With no way to know for sure, I shiver again, then turn my back on the church and shuffle along. I've spent enough time on the dead. Time to return to the business of the living and those caught in-between.

TWENTY-TWO

I make my way west, along the north bank of the river, no delays, no detours, no sightseeing. It's early afternoon when I cross Westminster Bridge and catch sight of County Hall. Nowhere has ever looked so inviting or felt so much like home, not even my old flat where I lived with Mum and Dad.

I don't hesitate. Ignoring the high-pitched noises coming out of the speakers dotted around the place – they deter normal zombies, but not a girl on a mission like me – I hobble down Belvedere Road, let myself into the building and make straight for Dr. Oystein's small lab, where the Groove Tubes are housed. I have a feeling I'll find him there, and I'm right. He's working on something when

I enter without knocking, running tests, studying the contents of a test tube.

The doctor doesn't look up, unaware that his privacy has been disturbed. I don't announce myself. Instead I strip and dump my clothes on the floor, then limp to the nearest Tube, smiling warmly at the thought of immersing myself and blissing out, of emerging whole and fresh in a few weeks.

There's a ladder close to the Groove Tube. I climb up and in. I hold on to the sides of the cylinder, half submerged. I think about saying nothing, grinning as I imagine the perturbed look on Dr. Oystein's face when he turns from his work later and spots me. But I can't hold my tongue.

"Doc," I call.

The doctor looks up and his eyes widen. *"B?"* he gasps.

I smirk at him, let go of the sides and slip beneath the surface of the liquid. As I'm falling, just before I go under, I shout out playfully—"I'm in!"

To be continued...